Guinevere and Lancelot

ZELKO SMITH

Copyright © 2016 Zelko Smith

Atrisco Press

All rights reserved.

ISBN: 1537225243
ISBN-13: 978-1537225241

Cover image from Geoffrey of Monmouth's Welsh edition of his *History of Britain*, 15th century.

CONTENTS

Preface   vii

Chapter 1   1

Chapter 2   7

Chapter 3   12

Chapter 4   16

Chapter 5   22

Chapter 6   30

Chapter 7   35

Chapter 8   49

Chapter 9   54

Chapter 10   64

Chapter 11   71

Chapter 12   75

Chapter 13   85

Chapter 14   88

Chapter 15   115

Chapter 16   148

Preface

The King Arthur-Lancelot-Guinevere legend is known, and so re-tellings of it tend to amplify its magnitude for dramatic appeal or provide as-yet-unknown details that flesh out new terrain. But the charm of the legend is that there are conflicting accounts, stories in multiple languages that over hundreds of years have become authentic and primary in themselves. This is where *Guinevere and Lancelot* fit in. The characters are here, the ones we expect, like King Arthur, Guinevere, Lancelot, Merlin, Gawain, Perceval, as are the adventures, like kidnapping, swordplay, and romantic intrigue. But unlike other stories, we have in *Guinevere and Lancelot* a departure into landscapes, psychology, and dialogue worthy of the legend. We get real anxiety, complacency, vanity, desperation. King Arthur sees his fate, knows he is helpless against it, and so seeks to erase his fate by accelerating through it. Lancelot's dynamism comes from how casual he is, how complacent, as he seems comfortable with being pinned down by his duty. And Guinevere, who finally gets proper attention, is not just a trophy to be won, but takes charge of her own destiny, finally.

ZELKO SMITH

Chapter 1

Guinevere, laughing and giggling, burst through the wooden gate so quickly that it swung back and forth, the slats cracking, pulling against the hinges, until its mooring post settled in a rooted furrow. Her sister, Maerwynn, stepped carefully in the mud, and her voice hiccupped when her dress got caught on the knotty spurs of the gate. Unhitching her laced flounce, she hurried to chase the swaying waves of Guinevere's golden hair. The fields around the outlying huts that surrounded the castle had recently been cleared of the corpses of fallen knights and soldiers. While the smell remained, the rotting horse carcasses had already been dragged away, as had the splintered and toppled provision carts that had been abandoned. Villagers, alongside King Leodegrance's errant boys in charge of battlefield cleanup, had already scavenged the arrows, plucking them from the breastplates of the dead, from the lifeless flesh of the decomposing horses, and from the damp earth, sodden with blood that pooled in the narrow ruts left by the retreating wagons. The blood, through much industry, had been plowed under, mixing with the grass and mulched shrubbery and soil, leaving the freshly tilled dirt fields ready for planting season.

Saplings were beginning to push up into the thick English air, heavy as it still was with the scent of rotting flesh. All the feral wildlife had been killed off to feed the troops. Only now were the cultivated pigs, those that could be corralled into the protective castle walls, starting to venture out from their pens to forage through the red mud for the new sweet sapling rootlets. The deer had scampered off, following the warblers and woodlarks. So too had the rabbits. The sheep and goats had all been slaughtered by the alien armies. Scattered were the cattle throughout the neighboring ravines. They were presently being gutted by the starving residents whose villages had been plundered and burned.

The forests had long since been pealed back toward the perimeters of the heath in the south and the wetland bogs to the north. Only patchy beech and bare broadleaf groves lined the horizon from the castle, save for the isolated twisted oak trees, much valued for the pockets of midday shade they provided. Replacing the vanished forests were meager orchards, now stripped and barren of both ripe and unripe fruit. The chestnut trees were picked clean, leaving the emerging villagers to search among the fluttering leaves for hidden chestnuts with which to make their porridge. Washed from the scene by the war were the purple gillyflowers and yellow gorse that the rocky outcroppings had protected from the livestock. Flowers that had survived grazing were trampled by the frantic, scurrying boots. The broadleaf tree branches that were cut down and used as camouflage to conceal troop numbers had been tossed aside when the orders were given. Slowly, the branches, snapped and chopped, were folded into the mud, sticky and black.

Guinevere's eyes were too much in the sunshine to notice the silhouettes of hunched-over peasants, with their hands plunged into the mud, feeling around for acorns beneath the oaks. She was happy to be free of the castle and felt the slip-sliding of her heels in the mud as her direct contact with the regeneration of the kingdom. Maerwynn called after her to slow down, and Guinevere paused at the top of a hill. She put her arms out wide, and the moist breeze fluted through the excesses of her dress. Rippling in the sporadic gusts were the fine silken folds of violet, curling around the contours of her legs. The citron billows that draped from her shoulders alternately swelled and compressed, serving as a kind of heralding for her coming of age, framed against the gray rolling clouds, for bright young Guinevere.

Maerwynn stood at the bottom of the hill, hidden from the breeze, staring in admiration, for Guinevere had always possessed a mature other-worldliness. Her child-like idealism mixed with her refined features. Like the clouds above, they were transient, wispy, but for the moment took shapes that ushered forth dreams of her life to come. And like the realism of the mud, at times overly convoluted, but authentic, they fashioned in them her visions of a genuine life one day. And recently, as if brought out by the wars the two sisters could only watch from the safety of the castle towers, she had added piercing beauty to the fairness of her manner. Maerwynn saw this now, in full bloom, Guinevere's beauty redeeming the human mulch on which they stood. But unlike Guinevere, whose aloofness held in it a bold confidence that Maerwynn hesitated to approach, she could only whisper to herself a spontaneous poem:

Annuals are bright, while perennials endure,
The first for flight, meant for amour,
The second for might and life is assured.

King Leodegrance, from his high tower in the castle, saw his daughters frolicking in the mud, running about, seemingly without a care for what had caused the destruction of his land. How could they run so freely, so blindly? He saw the two distant images, the girls, laughing and skipping about in circles, as being in their own world. Kingdoms take governance, take strategy, and without a male heir his two daughters would inherit his legacy. And do what with it, he thought. Perhaps he had been too lenient in their upbringing. If only their mother hadn't died giving birth to what would have been the proper heir. Without male heirs and his wife lost, opposing kings were given the very cause they needed for their long-standing intentions, for they saw this tragedy as a sign of weakness in the king. If he was unable to marshal his own fate, surly that was cause to doubt the very legitimacy of his reign. After all, how could a king with no son continue on, as the stability of the kingdom becomes superimposed over the mortality of the king? Surely a desperate endgame would ensue? What recourse did he have? He, of course, knew the price, and she was standing upon a hilltop with her arms outstretched. That was the price he had to pay for Arthur's help in the wars: the might of Camelot for Guinevere. He called a servant over.

"When Guinevere comes in, tell her I need to speak with her."

"Yes, your highness."

When Guinevere returned to the safe interiors of the castle, the servant directed her to her father's chamber. Without changing out of her soiled dress, she dutifully marched in her mud-covered boots down the hallway to the south wing to where the king was waiting. At the entrance to the chamber, the servant was a step late opening the door for her, and she unhesitatingly knocked three times, putting a little rhythm in her taps. Before the king could answer, she pushed it open.

"Father, a beautiful day. Not a soul in sight, but, oh, the breeze was blowing."

King Leodegrance got up and approached his daughter with the stern look of a father half-regretting the news he was about to deliver. But then he noticed her boots.

"Guinevere, what's that there?"

Looking down at the mud caked on her leather

boots, "Father, this dirt, do you not recognize your kingdom?"

While she got a light chuckle out of her phrase, the king realized the all-too-true nature of her question.

"No, I don't. I no longer recognize my kingdom. What you've seen, now multiply that by a hundred, by a thousand. It had been turned to mud, ground into a pulp by the years of warring. All that I have lost, the great knights, the townships burned, the treasure that poured out of my possession."

"Father, I didn't...."

She had realized her error.

"No, you are right. These wars cost me."

"But it's over. You won."

"I won the right to keep a broken kingdom. But whether now or one day, it was destined to be so. As you know, you have no brother, so I have no son. And with no son, no heir."

"I know."

"But there is a way." Guinevere felt her spirit lift, as hope would flutter all hearts. "As my first daughter, you may rule as queen."

"Me, queen?"

"But not here. You may rule my kingdom as Queen of Camelot."

"Camelot? Arthur's Camelot?"

"He is responsible for our land. He is the one who pledged his men, his greatest knights, who fought with us, for us. And now, Arthur may save our kingdom again. He has asked for your hand in marriage. And with it comes our land."

"I am to be married?"

"And Maerwynn is to go with you to serve, until she may find a husband of her own, as a maiden by your side."

Guinevere was both shocked and honored. She had never been to Camelot and had only seen Arthur from afar. Certainly she knew of his greatness, of his heroism, and if love hadn't yet appeared, the respect she had for him and all that he had done seemed equal to the task of winning her heart. She stood there in silence. Could reverence be a substitute for love? Could the duty of a daughter saving a kingdom be enough to fulfill her dreams of taming the clouds? Could she love Arthur? Guinevere, overwhelmed, knew what she had to say.

"Yes, I will marry Arthur for you."

"Oh, Guinevere, I dreaded telling you, but you have saved our family. The king sends his emissary tomorrow to accompany you and Maerwynn back to Camelot. And then I shall be along shortly for the wedding day."

He rushed to hug her, kissing her on each cheek and then on her forehead. King Leodegrance felt the weight of his old age, the weight of his deceased wife and child, the weight of the responsibility of his struggling kingdom, being lifted. He kept his arms around her, fighting back tears. She could feel him squeezing her shoulders. She could feel the thick mass of his royal vest and coat bearing down on her. She could feel the clouds taking shape.

Chapter 2

Guinevere and Maerwynn strolled together through the corridors of the castle. Guinevere was deep in thought, and her lingering at each turn held the two of them in space long enough for the squires lounging in the coves to steady their eyes on the golden-haired beauty.

"You walk slowly on purpose? To tease?" Maerwynn playfully asked Guinevere.

"To tease? Maerwynn, whoever would I be teasing? But listen, I have just had some news."

Before she could continue with the details of her impending marriage, they were approached by Rogerson, one of the more brash squires in the king's collection. He was handsome without being attractive, a uniquely hopeless quality, like a bouquet flowers presented without an eye for their arrangement.

"Would it seem the princess is lost in her own castle?" he said in full affectation.

Rogerson had all the effervescing character as was needed to intrude with a feeble opening script. Guinevere perked up. If Maerwynn was the poet, she was engaging in a slightly different way.

"Speaking here with you now, wouldn't I have to be lost?" A wry smile accompanied her words, not piercing but jousting. "So your comment is a double-edged sword, perceptive and yet how do you think it makes you appear?"

"Like spontaneously found treasure."

"Treasure?"

"Indeed, princess. A gift." He struggled to reach

into his cloak and pulled out a small bundle tightly wrapped in burlap. He slowly unwound the string binding to reveal a small vine nestled in a clump of soil. "May I present the princess with a raspberry vine for her collection? It has travelled from the far-reaches of a distant kingdom." Rogerson searched for a grander way to present it. "I believe it arrived by ship, or a vessel of some kind."

Guinevere took the vine into the palm of her hand and raised her eyebrows in mock puzzlement.

"A ship sailed in from a distant land-locked kingdom, you say?"

"Was it one of those new special land ships I have been hearing about?" Maerwynn added.

"Umm, or a vessel of some kind." Rogerson gathered himself, recognizing what the situation had become. "The princess has lovely way of accepting a gift."

"No, Rogerson. The real gift you gave me was the setup for my use of irony." He didn't get it. "The talk, I mean."

"You know my name?"

"And you call me lost?"

The sun had yet to set, but it was low enough for the castle walls to shield its rays from the inner private courtyard the king had allocated for Guinevere. When the wars had made venturing outside the gate too perilous, he had sectioned part of his personal courtyard as the official royal garden. And he had put Guinevere in charge. She turned the modest collection of grape vines and strawberry patches into what she called her "garden menagerie." As the years passed, she had requisitioned apple and orange trees, which she had positioned in front of the adjacent chapel windows in finely crafted pots. Dwarf lemon trees festooned the opposite perimeter, as did specially pruned peach and plum trees and rows of dwarf corn stalks. In between, she had rows of cranberries and cultivated cherry bushes beneath a hanging box of dangling cherry tomatoes. When the two apricot trees grew into one another, she had them twined together beneath a row of carrots. So alien at first were the pomegranates that when the king split the first one in half at dinner service, he dropped it in horror, and the girls giggled when he christened it the "devil berry fruit." The garden had become her own personal domain, to do with as she pleased. Guinevere treated it as a small kingdom of her own. She worked the soil and moved the pots and planter boxes inside during the winter months, and they, in turn, provided additions for the meals and desserts. This was her first try at governance. Her father, the king, had his lands and subjects, and she had hers. And now, one kingdom was alive and thriving. Maerwynn laid fresh soil down in a deep pot and delicately carved out a small hole into which Guinevere placed the raspberry vine.

The sun was setting now, and the evening torches were lit. The two sisters worked in the garden, watering, tending to the wayward branches and pruning.

"Isn't it nice we have this garden," Guinevere said.

"Yes. While the wars were ruining the land, it is as if we preserved the whole outside world."

"Almost. It is because we built this garden that we could allow the outside world to be ruined."

"So the men ruin it...."

"And this garden makes it so we can more easily stand by while they do. And then, when the time comes, we replace it."

"There's a funny kind of symbolism there," Maerwynn said, adjusting some stray rose blossoms that were drooping because they were too heavy for their stems.

"Hah, always with you poet's mind."

Maerwynn then passed with a small pair of shears,

and Guinevere grabbed her arm.

"For the peach tree," Maerwynn quickly said.

"No, something else. Come." And they both sat down on a bench overlooking the carpet of strawberries, now flickering black in the night. "Father has told me I am to be married to Arthur of Camelot."

"King Arthur?"

"Yes."

"And that would make you Queen."

"Of Camelot, yes. And you are to be my maiden."

"Me?"

"Yes. For the opportunities."

"Oh, Guin." Maerwynn hugged her with all her might. "That is wonderful. And we'll have a grand wedding."

"Yes, in Camelot."

"And a feast and a whole ceremony." Maerwynn saw Guinevere's apprehensive look and pulled back. "Do you want to marry Arthur?"

"I was told it was my duty, to help secure father's kingdom, to reward Arthur for his help in the wars."

"But you and I have dreamed of love. Would this be love?"

"Arthur is a great man. He is king. Love is only one reason for marriage. And I will be happy."

"Happiness is not love. In fact, they are opposites. Love is the best kind of horrible, terrible feeling. Love is like a war you wage on yourself, destroying everything."

"I have read your poems. You call love the willful embrace of destruction. I know."

"But queens do not destroy."

"That's right. I will be queen. But I do not know the first thing about being queen."

"I have only seen father be a king."

"That is true. I have never seen father be a queen," Guinevere said.

They were both quiet for a moment, during which Maerwynn noticed Guinevere's distant eyes and her apparent acquiescence. To insist on love, to force love, she thought, is to deny it.

"Guin, I wrote a line for one of my poems that says, A King is but a Queen, only less pretty. Except maybe a queen's hands wouldn't be so dirty."

Guinevere looked at the dirt in her nails and rubbed her soiled hands together. They both shared a resigned glance, and Maerwynn, with her poetic extrapolations, knew Guinevere's fate was sealed.

"And what else would you have me wash my hands of?" Guinevere said, trying to lighten the mood.

"Hah. But you should watch your phrases with Arthur. You think he values smartness in a queen?"

"I don't know. And what does he really know of me?"

"He knows you are beautiful."

"Beauty is but a form of smartness...only less pretty. Now come. Arthur sends his emissary to take us to Camelot tomorrow. We must be ready."

Chapter 3

The early morning sun shone through the distant emaciated trees and across the plowed fields, from which the decaying scent of rotting mulch drifted toward the waiting girls. In the wide gravel receiving yard, Guinevere and Maerwynn stood, along with a few servants to help with the trunks and bags.

"Now girls," King Leodegrance said, "the alliance will secure the legacy of this family, as it will join Arthur's kingdom and ours. He has fought hard for our safety, contributing many men and much treasure, so remember, respect above all else." The king's voice lightened. "Maerwynn, he has many valiant knights. Should one show an interest...."

"Father." She has heard all this before.

"Should one show an interest—I am only saying that your poetry would take an interesting turn. And Guinevere, you will be the most beautiful queen anyone has ever seen. The people of Camelot, and indeed all of England, are lucky to have you. So above all, respect."

"For Arthur or Camelot?" Guinevere said.

"And our garden," Maerwynn said, "you will tend to it?"

"I will," the king assured her.

From atop the castle wall, a trumpet sounded, announcing the arrival of the transport carriage.

"Now girls, look proper," their father said, and his daughters straightened their pose.

Four healthy steeds with knights hidden beneath their armaments trotted in through the portal. Then four more horses followed, carrying archers who were each complimented by a full quiver of arrows slung over their backs. After that, a three-horse team, one leading and two side-by-side, ushered forward the regal carriage. Four knights on horseback, two on either side, protected the coach at close range. Two archers were mounted topside, one at the rear and one beside the coachman. And then, atop spangled horses, six knights followed, covered head-to-toe in armor and each with a broad sword properly in its scabbard and ready.

The carriage swung round and came to a stop beside the girls. Out stepped a man, old, bearded, and covered in loose-fitting clothes, blue and purple and with gold stitching: Merlin. He stood there quietly. Next, a second man stepped down from the carriage, a knight, in full battle dress, all except the helmet. His orange and gray garments were loosely fitted, his shoulder plates protruding and giving him a much more imposing frame. He spoke with great enunciation.

"My name is Sir Kay. I am King Arthur's most trusted and faithful servant. King Leodegrance, these must be my two passengers. And which of you is Guinevere?" he asked, preparing a grand gesture of greeting.

Guinevere, with a slight tone, "If King Arthur is to have the most beautiful queen in all the land, wouldn't you be able to tell which of us be her?"

"Please excuse her, Sir Kay, I...," Leodegrance started to say.

Merlin stayed quiet, observing, and Sir Kay tried quickly to redeem himself.

"M'lady, the beauty of two sisters must never be compared."

Merlin then spoke softly.

"You are Guinevere," choosing correctly.

"And so you think her the more beautiful?"

Maerwynn said, smiling, not showing the customary deference to the austere Merlin.

"Maerwynn," King Leodegrance said, "please."

"No, it's quite all right," Sir Kay said. "This is Merlin. He is a wizard. And so surely he divined it."

Sir Kay was proud of his explanation, but was uncertain what to say next.

"No, no," Merlin laughed. "No sorcery here. Guinevere, you are certainly beautiful, but you are taller and," turning to Maerwynn and affecting a slight smile to indicate a joke, "clearly more mature and refined. But you two are sisters, and young Maerwynn, hearing you now, you will serve her well."

Maerwynn's lips broke into a sheepish smile, and she and Guinevere looked at each other to indicate a mutual affection for Merlin.

"They are their mother's daughters," King Leodegrance added, joining in the good-hearted conversation.

Sir Kay looked around awkwardly, struggling with what to say next.

"But I must say," he finally said, "as our schedule is tight, we must be off."

"Yes," King Leodegrance snapped and signaled to the servants, "Their belongings," and the servants quickly loaded the luggage onto the hind racks of the carriage.

As Merlin and Sir Kay awaited, Guinevere and Maerwynn hugged and kissed their father goodbye. Sir Kay opened the carriage door, and after the girls stepped inside, he said to King Leodegrance, "The wedding will be next month and Arthur with send word as to the exact date, as he eagerly awaits your arrival." Then Merlin gave a gentle bow, and the two of them boarded, quickly closed the door, and sat opposite the two girls. Sir Kay tapped on the roof with the ring on his finger, the coachman gave the reins a twitch, and they were off.

The royal entourage circled quickly around and disappeared through the portal. King Leodegrance gave a stern look, knowing he would miss his daughters but was glad to see his legacy and their safety would be secured. He then turned his servants.

"The girls' garden, have it broken down and replanted in the fields." The servant balked at the order. "It's for everyone now. It's what they wanted."

Chapter 4

The rumbling horses and the knights and archers moving around in their saddles made for reassuring noises for the girls. True silence would have been awkward. They looked out the window and tried to guard their expressions, for they had never seen the countryside so devastated. Guinevere had to sit back and look away, appalled as she was at the uprooted and toppled and splintered trees, the smoldering fires, the rubble of piled stones and straw that had been houses. But after a moment, she sat forward again and looked out the window. Merlin saw this.

"You know," he said, "the fleeing soldiers, their marching flattened the road, giving us a smooth ride."

"And a smooth ride is a boring ride," Sir Kay said out into the air, to no one in particular. Perhaps he was feeling a little put out by being reduced to the role of escort. Although stealing glances at the pretty young Guinevere was fine to pass the time.

"Father never told us what the war over," Guinevere said.

"What did we win?" Maerwynn said.

"Honor. Pride," Sir Kay quickly said and made a subtle motion to Guinevere as if to assure her.

And then Merlin corrected him.

"The right to live as we have been living. You, we, were invaded, and so it was fought to hold onto what we have."

"Defensive, then." Guinevere figured military matters were now hers to concern herself with.

"Not exactly," Merlin said, but then said no more.

When there was a moment of silence, Maerwynn took her eyes from the window.

"Maybe the war was fought to stave off boredom," she said and shrugged.

Sir Kay was angered by her lack respect for the death of others.

"You are a princess. What do you know of war?"

"Perhaps Maerwynn is right in one aspect," Merlin said. "We may discover why wars are waged, but we can ever know why one fights."

"Princess," Sir Kay continued, "you may pretend to know of war, but you do not. Because of boredom? At least your sister here has the good sense to ask questions rather than spout theories," and with that he nodded to the queen-to-be. "Guinevere, is this what you would like to talk about, war?"

"Enough," Merlin said. "Sir Kay, you seek war here in this carriage to defeat the boredom of this trip, is that so?"

"And," Maerwynn added, "you ask my sister a question so that you may have a reason to stare at her unashamedly as she talks, is that so?"

Sir Kay let out a huff and looked out the window. Guinevere's faint apologetic expression as if she had done something wrong did not satisfy Maerwynn, who further raised her eyebrows to try to convince her sister of Kay's secret glances. But the gap in understanding remained. All of this was to Merlin's growing sorrow, for he saw Guinevere's innocence as being a far more dangerous trait than Maerwynn's confrontational nature.

"When you meet the rest of the knights, especially the ones of the Round Table," Sir Kay said to both Maerwynn and Guinevere, "be sure to be as honest as you are now."

"What is the Round Table?" Guinevere asked.

"You know the table was a gift from you father," Merlin said.

"The very best of the best of the knights, your husband's select protectors of Camelot. Be sure to tell them what you think of their bloodshed."

"Sir Kay," Merlin said, trying to halt the knight's words. Sir Kay quieted down, and Merlin tried to reassure the girls. "Maerwynn, I promise you, you will never be bored. And Guinevere, yes, all wars are defensive, on both sides, for aggression is always a defensive act."

As the carriage rolled through the great heath, the sunlight, unobstructed now, warmed the coach, and Guinevere leaned into the warmth. Soon they approached the boundaries of the kingdom of Camelot, and soon Camelot, the formal fortification itself, spread out over the vast incline of a large rolling hillside. Framed by its encircling walls, the castle seemed a centerpiece on a table setting. The stone walls glistened in the sun, sparkling as if freshly polished. Its spires, piercing up through the clouds, were as candles setting the romantic mood of its citizens, its gentry, its knights, and the king who had the wedding preparations underway. Servants were sent far and wide to retrieve flowers. Hunters and trappers selected from the king's private reserve the plumpest pigs and finest venison to roast.

Such was the scene Guinevere was anticipating, eager to get to Camelot. But Maerwynn thoughts were directed in the other direction, at the lives they were leaving. Newness was always strange to her. Pensive, meditative, brooding at times, wrapped up in rethinking past events, as this was the natural process of the overwrought mind of a poet, she realized the loss her old life meant the loss of what grounded her. And Camelot, bright and exciting as it was, was a projection of uncertainty and mystery, hardly the fodder for Maerwynn's rough-edged personality. Unlike Guinevere who Maerwynn saw as somewhat dependent on the appreciation of others, which is why the marriage proposal was all that was needed to sustain her projections of physical stability despite the recognized absence of love, she needed the foundation of enduring memories to prop up her feelings of security. Especially for someone as confrontational as Maerwynn. In a place in which she had yet to establish herself, her assertiveness and sense of belonging had no foundation. Knowing this, and not knowing her place in Camelot, she had yet to figure out how to avoid becoming the castle annoyance, buzzing about. She wanted to fit in and belong without getting in the way, and with her sister being the new center of attraction, the prospect of becoming a kind of sentimental sideshow frightened her.

As the carriage arrived, the hustle of the kingdom sent Guinevere to entertaining the idea as to whether she was worth the attention. Indeed, how had she earned the wedding or the right to feel special? By virtue of her good acts? No. They seemed merely a birth right, conferred upon her because of her beauty, not by her virtue. It was then she figured her first duty as queen was to live up to the contours of her face and the sleekness of her hair. This was the first time she had sought the right to earn her beauty.

Amid these thoughts, the carriage passed a small sporting arena where men were engaged in sword play. At least that's how Guinevere saw it, as play, with a crowd cheering after each wave and clash of the metal. A game, she thought, and the jousting was pointless but was interesting in its rules and resets. Maerwynn flinched and cringed along with the crowd after the clangs and blows, and was impressed by the fluid sword movements. It was both graceful and powerful, and as the carriage moved out of view of the tournament, she stuck her head out of the window to catch further glimpses of the knights.

A small receiving party—four undistinguished

knights and a battery of servants and custodial staff—at the north wing of the castle had been sent to welcome Guinevere and Maerwynn. After pleasant introductions and bowing,
and after Merlin and Sir Kay went their separate ways, a young, almost pretty girl stepped forward.

"I am Victoria, and I am to escort you to your chambers. Arthur thought it best to meet his new queen for the first time alone so as not to disorient you with regard to the proper mix of emotions and protocol."

Victoria delivered her message with a professional tone. She was a little older than the girls, and her years of belonging to king's retinue had ingrained in her a strict adherence to the conventions of proper decorum. Older, yes, but still young, and Maerwynn and Guinevere both saw in her a new, if uninitiated ally in Camelot.

While the girls were shown their rooms, Merlin took a different door, then another, climbed some stairs, and found King Arthur out on a balcony overlooking his land.

"M'lord, they have arrived."

"I heard." Arthur was pensive, as if lost in reverie, and looked more worried than excited. "I know, Merlin, I know," he said, as if talking of something else.

"We both know. And meeting with her now, I have confirmed these thoughts. They are true."

"But...."

"But you will marry her still," Merlin said, already knowing the answer.

"Because I'm in love."

"When we went to war to aid King Leodegrance, we knew we'd lose men, but we did it because it was the right thing to do."

"Or in order for me to extract this favor. Maybe that was it."

There was a pause, and both men knew the truth, what the truth was then and what the truth would be.

"The wedding will be beautiful," Merlin said.

Arthur adjusted his crown, making sure it was straight. He drifted back into reverie.

"You know, Merlin, some of my explorers just returned from The East, and I was told this parable. A man was struggling to make his way through the jungle, so tangled was the undergrowth, so thorny were the vines, when he came upon a Leopard. Suddenly, as he was running, with the Leopard in pursuit, pathways in the dense jungle seemed to open up for him, ones he had never seen before."

"Yes, from The East. And when the Leopard chased him up a peach tree and followed him out onto a limb, and a serpent coiled on the branch above him, and a tiger had wandered over and stared up at him from below, the man reached out, plucked a peach, and took a bite—delicious."

Chapter 5

Camelot, during the lead up to the wedding, involved more than just preparations for the pageant marriage. The days were also spent getting Guinevere and Maerwynn used to their new lifestyle. They were taken around in the coach and given the tour of the kingdom by Merlin, who pointed out such things as how the bog was drained to make room for farmland, the nuances of village architecture, how the market worked. Accompanying Guinevere and Maerwynn on these excursions was Victoria, and she was slowly becoming part of the group. They, at times, when Guin would see a point of interest, would have the carriage stop, and they'd all get out. Sometimes it was to talk to a village member, where Guin would pat the children on the heads and Maerwynn would look at a copy of an old book they might have on their shelves, for few could read. Or Merlin would inquire as to what kind of vegetables they had planted in their gardens, which was always taken as an implicit request to sample some of the new carrots or cherry tomatoes. Thus, they filled their early days, while Arthur was back at the castle tending to political matters, seeing the kingdom.

The girls would exchange humorous comments about Merlin's wardrobe, how he always wore loose robes with baggy sleeves and how his beard was so disheveled. And Victoria would add to Merlin's stories. The girls found especially funny the tales of young squires trying to become knights, hearing how they would struggle to lift the broad swords that were too heavy for them or try and joust, only to have their lances, after the long gallop, dragging on the ground when it was time for impact. And the girls would laugh. Even Merlin, who was normally weighed down by the affairs of the state, found himself caught up in their storytelling. As they continued their tour in the coach, he shared the tale of the timid knight who was so overly-cautious that he built a shield the exact size of his body so that he may hide the whole of himself behind it.

"What about the brave knights?" Guinevere wondered.

"It is paradox," Merlin explained. "The ones who tell the most harrowing tales of danger and courage, how do the villagers know if what they say is true? And the ones who don't say anything, do they really have nothing to report, or are they modest?"

"Then how can you know?" Maerwynn asked.

"Look at their armor and sword and shield. Look for blood. And the best knights, their pieces of armor don't match, because they take the best of what they can find off those they kill. So, a hint, if you ever see a knight with clean, polished, glittering armor, you will know he is not a true warrior." Guinevere nodded. "But that is only true for most, for the best knights are the exceptions."

"What do you mean?" Maerwynn asked.

"Knights often try to look impressive so as to intimidate others, so they never have to prove themselves in battle. But the true knight lets his skill not his appearance win the day. Except when his skill is his appearance."

"Oh, Merlin," Victoria interrupted, "how come with you, if one thing is true, then the opposite is also always true, and often times more true?"

Merlin shrugged. The carriage rode on.

As the days passed and the wedding day drew closer, tailors and seamstresses came to the castle with different dresses for Guinevere to choose from. They'd line up and Guin would go inspect each dress, running the fabric through her fingers, holding up the tulle in front of the light, tugging at the seams to test its structure. She'd try a few on, posing in front of the mirror, take pointers from Maerwynn and Victoria. The seamstresses were so proper in their deference, always agreeing with the girls' criticisms. Until, that is, one woman, with a humble hunch of the shoulders, said, after Victoria had made a comment as to the width of a waistband, "But that would make the queen appear to be wider than she is. Perhaps these vertical panels of white, here, on my dress, might be more flattering." Guinevere nodded and went over to her dress, looking at the panels of fabric she was talking about. And then, after trying it on, Victoria said, "I agree with her." And Maerwynn said so, too. And Guin, twirling in the dress, as the train wound around her, said very calmly, "I have found my dress." She then went over to the grateful woman and asked if she'd make Maerwynn's and Victoria's dresses as well.

Maerwynn, in her travels with Merlin, had become fascinated with the glassworks of the kingdom. At every market and outpost, she would make a special detour to search out new glassware, some new little container or holder with varying contours. Soon, she had collected bottles of all kinds and colors: emerald green bottles with rigid panels that had been used to store medicinal elixirs, small rose-colored vases with openings like curled flower petals, opaque jars with hazy-white designs, bottles fused with the mist of smoked honey—she collected them all. And in her chamber, on special shelves of glazed sandalwood built by the royal carpenter, she arranged them all: by color, by size, by what they had contained in their former uses—arranged in front of the wide east-facing window so that as the sun rose in the morning and the light pierced through the chromatic glass, scattered rainbows cast themselves on the cold stone walls which surrounded her bed. So that each day, after her dreams of distant lands and noble knights, she awoke to such dizzying arrays of colored light that she often thought she were still in a dream. Then she would stay in bed and watch the dust the morning breeze had stirred filter through the rainbows, bringing the light into even more dazzling relief. And then she'd roll over and pull out from under her bed the small chest in which she kept her stack of papers on which she wrote her poetry. In slow contemplation, she'd compose various poems, at times writing them out quickly and at times with slow deliberation. She imagined that the light that spread itself over her papers infused itself into her poems, imparting in them, she believed, a mystical quality that gave her writing both a depth and timelessness. This was the imaginative part of her life, full of consequences, literary to be sure, so different from the day-to-day mediocrity that she felt flooded peaceful Camelot.

As all writers seek to be more than writers, and all poets seek to live out the dramas they merely draft on the page, Maerwynn secretly longed for the days when the wars were being waged. There, when the swords clashed, was drama, passion, the quickening of life that made the heart pound to a music that peacetime had now slowed to a numbing waltz wrought with complacency and forced distraction. Her newly-started writing lessons had forced her to confront these moods, which were always present but only now had she begun to put them into words. There, laying in bed, as the rainbows cast themselves over her sheets, her papers, and even Maerwynn herself, she was presently trying to express the otherwise untamed contours of love. After a few tries at trying to find the right vocabulary, only to scratch these efforts out in frustration, she realized she didn't know about love firsthand. What other poets had written she was well familiar with, but herself, what did she know? The red sunbeams on her wrist baffled her. What did they actually mean? She kicked her sheets off and went to find Guinevere.

Guinevere stood out on the low balcony and looked into the courtyard, a wide rectangular expanse with arched passageways at either end. A flock of small girls where running around, taking turns chasing each other in circles, and all Guinevere could think was how bald and fleshy their knees where, how exposed. It would merely take one stumble and fall, and the stone ground of the courtyard would tear into their skin. No longer did her thoughts drift into imagining the freedom the girls were enjoying, nor did their giggles and laughter find an echo in her own response to their playing. Instead, she went right into what she could only term her queenly role, that of concerning herself with how fragile the girls were and how protective she had become, as if burgeoning inside her was an awkward motherly instinct.

Guinevere suddenly felt very uncomfortable watching the girls skip and swing their arms around and lift their faces up to the heat of the sun. Across the courtyard an elderly woman was tending to some weeds that were pushing up through the cracks in the stones, in an out of the way area where more foot traffic would have kept the weeds down. Between the elderly woman, with her sweat seeping through the collar of her blouse as she strained to reach down and violently twist the weeds from their foundations, and the girls' twirling and their faces glistening with youthful perspiration, the new queen could only reflect on the lost world of her childhood.

As her mind was lost the maze of alien thoughts, she turned her palms up and looked at the white purity of her skin. The broad stone balcony railing in front of her was unpolished and retained its course rough-cut texture. Reaching out, she placed her hands on the railing and slowly dragged them along, letting the coarse stone scrape her palms, not violently, not to bloody them, but to put subtle white striations on her otherwise innocent hands. Then she turned them over and rubbed them together. Bringing her hands up to inspect the changes, she saw that nothing had happened. Her skin was as smooth and soft as ever. To make sure, she placed her hands on her cheeks, but could feel only their warm silkiness. Nothing had changed.

Maerwynn came out on the balcony and startled Guinevere.

"What are you doing out here?" She said and stepped out to the edge to look over into the courtyard.

"Where else am I supposed to be?" Guinevere said with a kind of wistful look that Maerwynn noticed and then quickly dismissed.

"My lesson, I learned some new stuff. We worked on metaphor."

"Oh, that's nice."

Guinevere's thoughts were elsewhere, and her sister, rather than pursue her feelings, tried to create new ones in her sister. It was something her poet's mind had learned at an early age.

"Maybe you can help me." She held up her papers. "For next time, I have to come up with what love is like, different metaphors for what love is like."

Guinevere didn't have the courage to tell her sister that she had no clue what love is like, for she had yet to fall in love with Arthur. Respect and awe for his crown and the royal seal had not translated into love, and she was starting to doubt if it ever would.

"Maerwynn, I don't know?"

Her sister, never at a loss for words, puzzled over this, Guinevere's inability to describe love and her admission that, in effect, she was not in love with

Arthur.

"You don't know? How can you not know?"

"Let me explain. On the carriage ride to Camelot I formulated a simple way to figure out if I was in love: to ask myself two questions. Are my feelings new? I've had mild feelings before, and if none of my romantic feelings escalated above how I have felt before, then it's not love. But to guard against being overwhelmed by all this, the ceremonies, the attention, I thought that if I was able to put my feelings into words, then it wouldn't be love either."

"I don't understand. I just spent a whole lesson talking about writing about love, about finding words for it."

"That's wrong, because love isn't like anything. Part of the courage of saying you're in love is the courage to also say you're at a loss to describe it. It's a feeling unlike, well, anything you might have written down on that paper."

"But we talked about love for an hour, and we said plenty of words?"

"Maerwynn, have you ever been in love?"

"No."

"Well then, how do you know what love is like?"

Maerwynn took these words as an accusation. She was the poet, the one who prided herself in knowing and writing down her feelings. And now she was just told all her thoughts on love were unfounded. Anger overtook her, partly because she knew her sister was right.

"What I do know is that if I was given the chance to love a king, I would. Your failure at love is not love's fault. You say you can't describe love in order not to fall in love. You say don't know it in order not to find it."

And with that Maerwynn stormed off and Guinevere's calling after her did no good. She was alone again on the balcony. The girls below in the courtyard where gone, but the gardener was still there, the elderly woman, still laboring to keep the grounds free of weeds. Guinevere again looked at her hands, again seeing how white and soft they were.

"Love is like.... Love is like.... Love is like...," came a voice from behind Guinevere. It was Maerwynn, with a kind tone, returning to smooth things over. Guin turned around to face her.

"Maerwynn is like.... Maerwynn is like.... Maerwynn is like...."

"You're right. I don't want to be compared to anything."

Chapter 6

The wedding day had arrived, and, with King Leodegrance in attendance, King Arthur and Queen Guinevere were to be married. Before the gathering crowd, a red velvet stage was set up, canopied in festooned white flowers. On the side of the stage were the royal trumpeters playing fleet-footed melodies. Gold-tasseled banners were waving from the posts. The sun was in its place. Merlin preformed the ceremony in front of the adoring crowd. Beneath hanging flowers, with the reception set for the royal courtyard where the pigs and venison were roasting, the villagers stood in awe of their new queen. How beautiful she was, how other-worldly, with her white veil pulled back and the long train of her dress escorted along by Maerwynn—although Guinevere felt uncomfortable looking so glamorous, so much the spectacle. The white veil was enough, but her dress, as Guinevere thought, was overly beautiful: the diamond-encrusted neckline, the vertical seams garnished with emeralds, the veins within the white silk spangled with gold—beautiful because of its strangeness, because no one had ever seen anything like it before. And the villagers marveled, happily, at the pageantry. Merlin looked over the crowd and saw how calm they were, how they seemed, for the first time since the wars, to enjoy living in Camelot. All seemed right. Guinevere was star struck, in part by her own glamorous appearance, and in part by the fuss that was being made over her. And so she stood there, on the constructed velvet stage, surrounded by strings of purple and gold flowers, in front of all the nobles, her father and sister, in front of the townsfolk, listening to the various regal pronouncements, not knowing where she was to fit in. What does queen mean?

Yet for all the flowers and smiles, for all the tables of food and guests of honor, a strange thought crept into Guinevere's mind: not the idea of marriage, but the idea of her marriage, obligated as she was to enter into an obligation, that of a matrimonial union. But rather than feeling the heaviness of such a burden, she felt relieved. And so she stood there, beside Arthur, in the front of the priest, with a complete lightness of being. There, as the center of attention, she felt weightless, as though held up by the wings of angels. Why? Because she wasn't in love. Love, she thought, would cloud her mind, would reshuffle her priorities, would confuse her. Love would push others away. Love would make her act selfish, as she would pursue only her desires, forsaking all other responsibilities. It would make her act brashly, foolishly, blindly. Love would ruin her. But here, with Arthur, in a marriage void of any real romantic feelings, let alone love, she could remain free, unfettered by such emotional entanglements. Suddenly, she became focused again. It was clear. Not wife to Arthur, but queen to Camelot.

After the formal wedding, after the reception, after being congratulated by acquaintances and strangers, after Guinevere's father had left, she found herself in her chamber exchanging her wedding dress for a more simple and comfortable gown. Arthur entered and silently went over to her armoire and picked out a different dress.

"Do I really need all this?" Guinevere said, looking at what Arthur had selected and trying to smooth down all the elaborate folds and loose fabric. She put the gown on over her slip, and Arthur leaned over to help arrange the billows.

"A queen must look the part."

"But I am not going to receive any more people today, am I? Let me play queen tomorrow."

"You are always the people's queen, even behind closed doors. And perhaps you are dressing to receive something else. Perhaps a gift."

Arthur reached beneath his coat and pulled out a small box.

"Oh. Well then, let me fix my dress. Do I know what it is?"

Guinevere smiled and assumed the more regal stance. Suddenly her dress became appropriate.

"You may guess," Arthur said, keeping the box close to his coat.

"A hint, please."

Arthur moved in near enough to whisper and slowly began his words as if reciting a poem.

"It is from the king. It is not a ring. It is on a string...."

"Pearls," Guinevere quietly shouted, giddy and excited.

Arthur hung his head.

"Ah, you guessed it."

"Have I, have I?"

"And now you have taken all the fun out of giving it to you."

Guinevere noticed a hint of resignation in her husband, full of dejection and defeat. Gone were his wide eyes. They were now replaced by a look alien to Guinevere, a look seeming to give away a whole emotional world she had never seen before. She spoke softly.

"There's still fun in it, sure. Let me see."

"I cannot. Because you have guessed my gift, I can no longer give it to you. You have turned my gift into a promise."

Guinevere now could not tell whether Arthur was

serious or not.

"A king could certainly make a simple promise to his queen?" she said.

"Nothing will ever be simple."

"But surely a gift...?"

"Now that you expect it, you have turned it into an obligation. And a king should not be obligated in such a way."

Guinevere was puzzled.

"So you give gifts not because of how they may make the receiver feel, but because of how they make you feel. Is that what giving a gift means to you?"

Arthur's tone became paternal.

"For a king it is different. The exchange is for your surprise and gratitude. Now, it is one-sided."

"You give me pearls as a king? Give them to me as my husband."

"You call me king or husband—when it suits you."

There was still a soft tone in Arthur's voice. He knew there was no point in arguing. Guinevere stepped back a few feet.

"There you are my king." She then moved forward. "And here you are my husband," and she kissed him.

Arthur was pleasantly amused at her display.

"Is this how you secure your gifts?"

She kissed him again.

"This is how I secure our marriage."

Arthur looked away.

"Did you see the villagers today? They were.... Something was wrong."

"They looked peaceful, just fine, happy."

"Yes, doesn't that disturb you?"

"Not at all. And the wars are over. They should rejoice."

"With the wars over, they look to their own problems, and then to me."

"What are their problems?"

"Ah, Guinevere, what do I know of being poor, of

being a...villager? These jousting and sword tournaments can only distract them for so long."

Guinevere sensed uncertainty rather than the arrogance of an out-of-touch monarch, and her pragmatic side came out.

"Then tomorrow, I shall go to the village and find out."

"But you are the queen now, and the queen can't just go out unprotected. They have all seen you."

"Then I shall go in disguise. Let this be my first duty as your queen. And I shall take Maerwynn and Victoria, and we will learn what is troubling them."

Arthur thought for a moment, and his face contorted from worried to a resigned powerlessness.

"OK, but that will not be your first duty as queen."

"Oh. What will?"

Her innocence and naiveté the king took as a joke, for this was to be their wedding night. He kissed her and smiled.

"You win," he said.

Chapter 7

The night had given way to day, and all artifacts of yesterday's wedding had been washed away by the bright morning sun. Two knights were walking along a country road, following the line of shade provided by a row of trees.

"But look at your sword, plain. Look at mine." This was Sir Gawain, the king's nephew. He unsheathed his sword and held it out for display. "You see the notch work around the hilt, here? The symmetry. Look at this on the handle, the finest imported rubber. When it gets hot, the rubber gets sticky and counteracts the sweat. Secures my grip."

"What is rubber? But how is your skill?"

"Doesn't matter. War's over. The new skill of a knight is in how he looks."

"But what good is that?"

"To impress women. Did you see Guinevere at the wedding?"

Smiles broke out over each of their faces.

"I could never get someone like her," Perceval said. "Who could?"

The road wandered on, with isolated oak trees dotting the horizon and fields of trampled brown grasses flickering in the breeze. The fields were quiet, except for a fly buzzing around Sir Lancelot's head. He was trying to catch up on his sleep, not that he was in need, but it was a good way to pass the time. So he swatted in front of his face while trying to keep his eyes closed. He had shifted his sword over, so as not to roll over on it, and had propped his feet up on his shield. He enjoyed his solitude. Unlike other knights, who were always feeling compelled to demonstrate their prowess with the sword or their riding abilities, he had the quiet confidence of a man who trusted in his will. Growing up in France, his uncle had tutored him in the ways of being a knight, and so hard and often did he train that he now relied not on his skills but on his determination, on his will. And this is why he slept, because he could.

"Lancelot, that you?" he heard from down by the road. Gawain's voice carried, and Lancelot sat up. "We're going into the market to pick up maidens. You, too?"

"I'm going for the food," Perceval yelled after him. Gawain looked at Perceval as if to indicate that there was no difference between food and women. Seeing Gawain's quizzical look, "I'm hungry," Perceval quietly said.

"Well, me, too," he replied, and then shouted up to Lancelot, "We're both hungry."

Gawain and Perceval waited down by the road. Lancelot took one last swat at the fly, brushed himself off, and joined the two other knights.

"You weren't at the wedding," Gawain said to Lancelot.

"Yes, I didn't see you there," Perceval added.

"Right," he answered.

As they walked on toward the market—they had a ways to go—Gawain thought Lancelot's response not good enough.

"And?"

"And what?"

"Why weren't you there?"

Lancelot thought for a moment.

"I don't know. Guess I don't have a reason."

"Arthur's going to be mad."

"You should have seen her, Queen Guinevere," Gawain said, almost drifting into reverie. "Like an angel, spangled in color, young but mature, hair like the strands of molten gold."

"Don't we have a Round Table meeting tonight?" Perceval asked.

"Excuse me, I was talking about the queen," Gawain insisted.

"Do we have a meeting?" Lancelot said. "I never know."

"Yes, early evening. And fine, you'll just have to meet Guinevere yourself," Gawain said. "And there's supposed to be some reforms. Knights with no war, he's going to do something."

"What? Hold another tournament? It's a distraction, I understand, but it's a distraction none the less."

Lancelot's perceptiveness was lost on Perceval.

"What do you mean?"

"He means," Gawain said, "that a warrior with no war turns inward and then fights inward."

"The goal is to fight inward first, win, and then turn outward," Lancelot added.

They walked on. The market was still around the next bend in the hillside, and Perceval decided to revisit Gawain's theory of attraction.

"Gawain, tell Lancelot about your sword."

"Yes. I was saying earlier that my sword here, like the designs around the edges of my breastplate and my polished boots, serve to impress the maidens."

"So, they'll be interested in you because they're interested in your shiny boots? I don't understand," Perceval said.

Lancelot was quiet. Gawain continued.

"It's about gaining a sexual advantage. Given the competition, everything gets appraised. My boots, why does it matter if they are polished or if there are little embellishments on the clasp, and so forth? They're for battle, for fighting. Glistening metal can't kill people. So why do it?"

"Pride? Tradition? Intimidation on the battlefield?" Perceval said.

"No. To attract women. Everything not immediately useful has its roots in gaining favor with the opposite sex. Look at the great blue red-beak, how it puffs its throat out and shows its excessive plume of bright feathers. Surely, that runs counter to him finding food and avoiding predators. Right? So, it's for the women."

"Ah, I see," Perceval said.

"Seems like a lot of effort," Lancelot said. "Sir Gawain, you are a romantic."

"Yes, I am. And to prove that's how it works, Perceval, when we get to the market, you will begin these very prescribed ways of systematic seduction."

"I would like to see that," Lancelot said.

"Oh, I don't know." Perceval was immediately nervous.

On the other side of the market, behind a clump of trees, Maerwynn further rumpled Guinevere's dress and brushed some dirt over it, while Victoria was busy pinning Guinevere's hair back and hiding it under a tightly-wrapped veil.

"Any of that hair gets out and they'll know it's her," Maerwynn said.

"I know, I know," Victoria said, "but I don't think this is a good idea."

"We'll be fine," said Guinevere.

"Yes, people are people," Maerwynn added.

"But you are the queen, and you a princess," Victoria objected.

But Guinevere, determining she was ready, walked out from behind the trees, and Maerwynn gave Victoria a glance before they hurried to catch up to her. With the three of them in disguise, they were sure no one notice who they were.

"Now," Guinevere said, taking charge, "we need to

observe, and if people talk to us, we engage them. Nothing too much, but we need to find out what the general sentiment is toward the king."

The market was full of villagers selling their wares, with a butcher's shop nearby, a man selling rugs from distant kingdoms across the way, with small hens and chickens running around freely. Maerwynn tried to look into the pottery booth, but no one was there. Victoria, as a vegetable cart went by, was busy making sure Guinevere was covered up. This was a nice outing for Guinevere, taking the initiative as she was, making independent strides toward her own identity as queen. She caught a glimpse of herself in a mirror and liked that she could barely recognize herself. Her natural looks had all but disappeared, and she felt free to be who she really was, not trapped by her beauty. Her disguise allowed her to be her true self. And Maerwynn saw this in how her sister walked and in how casually she ran her hand along the silk scarves that hung from the post outside a shop.

"It's fun to dress down," Maerwynn said.

"But did we have to go so far as to put dirt beneath our fingernails?" Victoria said.

"We, my sister and I," Guinevere said, "used to have a garden, and father was always telling us to wash our hands because our nails were so dirty."

"And he was right," Victoria quickly said.

"Maerwynn, how about a spontaneous poem about dirty nails."

Maerwynn thought for a moment.

"A warning: those who do not have dirt on their nails often, will soon have dirt on the nails of their coffin."

"How does that make sense?" Victoria objected.

"Well, it rhymes so it must be true," Guinevere said, and the girls laughed not the giggle of youth but the mature chuckle that was brought about by wit.

"So, you see that damsel over there?" Gawain pointed out. They had entered the market, and the plan for proving Gawain's theory of courtly love was being tried.

"Where?" Perceval said.

"There, alone. You see?"

Lancelot stood by, watching this charade. Gawain had picked out a girl who was fairly pretty and shopping alone.

"What do I do?" Perceval asked.

"Just stare at her until she notices you."

"Ok," and he fixed his gaze.

"Wait, wait," Gawain said quietly, as if this whole plan was based on timing. "There, you see? She sees you."

Indeed, the maiden had spotted Perceval, and she blushed, as if on cue. Then, slowly, she took out her handkerchief and delicately dropped it on the ground.

"You see, you see," Gawain said. "Now, go over and pick it up and give it back to her. Then give her some flowers, and if she accepts them, gently kiss her on the back of the hand, find out her name, and come back. Simple."

"Perceval, just talk to her. You're a nice guy," Lancelot said, weary of all this.

"No. We have a plan. Follow it through," and with that, Gawain gave him a light push on his shoulder to send him on his way.

Gawain and Lancelot watched Perceval shuffle over to the maiden. But as he leaned over to pick up her handkerchief, he stumbled and with his hand shoved it further into the dirt and smeared it with mud. Then, regaining his poise, he presented her with her filthy crushed handkerchief and bowed. She stood still, completely perplexed. Then, trying to fill the silence, Perceval made an awkward lunge at a flower cart, clutched a bouquet, and pushed it into her hand.

The man whose cart he robbed called out to him. Petrified, the girl held her grimy handkerchief in one hand, the bouquet in the other. Perceval, at loss, seeing that she held onto the flowers, reached for her flowered hand and aggressively kissed it and kissed it and kissed it and wouldn't stop. By this time, the flower merchant, with his yelling, had gotten Perceval's attention, and Perceval dropped her hand and looked her in the eyes. "What's your name? What's your name?" he kept saying. Then, with the merchant bearing down on him, he ran, running back toward Gawain and Lancelot. "See you tonight at the Round Table," he called out as he ran passed, with the merchant giving chase. Gawain and Lancelot burst into laughter, not at Perceval's expense, but at the whole scene. Then Gawain approached the girl.

"I'm not sure what that was about, but can I interest you in something to eat? Have you had lunch yet?" And with that Gawain extended the palm of his hand, the girl took it, and they walked off. Gawain looked back at Lancelot, shrugged, and ran his hand down the length of his sword as if that was the key to securing the girl on his arm. Lancelot shook his head and smiled.

Alone now, Lancelot saw a group of three women milling about and, deciding he had nothing better to do, made his way over to them. The tall one in the center caught his eye.

"Excuse me, may I present the fair maiden with a flower?"

Victoria, resorting back to protocol, "Fair maiden? You will address her—"

Guinevere stopped her.

"This fair maiden would be delighted to accept a flower."

Maerwynn found this entertaining. Lancelot turned his head back toward the flower merchant and made sure all three women saw what he was looking at. Then he stepped beside Guinevere and plucked a simple blossom from the ground and presented it to her.

"A flower for the fair maiden."

Guinevere graciously accepted it.

"You would present a woman with a weed?" Victoria protested.

"I beg your pardon, but you would call a flower christened by the king's soil a weed?"

"The king would be very pleased to hear you say that," Guinevere said.

Maerwynn was impressed by her sister's composure.

"Ah, you know what pleases the king?" he said.

"I might...perhaps..."

"But does he know what pleases you?" Lancelot said, amused, but when Guinevere looked puzzled, "You, a loyal subject. Does the king know what would please one of his subjects?"

"I don't think the king's business is appropriate for discussion," Victoria said.

"Well," Lancelot said to Guinevere, not looking at Victoria, "what would you like to discuss?" He then glanced confidently at Maerwynn, who approved of the whole situation.

"Would you excuse me," Guinevere said, and pulled both Victoria and her sister away by the elbow. She whispered to them. "This might be a good chance to see how a real person feels. Why don't you let me talk to him alone?"

And then, without waiting for a response, she went back to Lancelot. Victoria started to object, but Maerwynn grabbed her by the arm. "She is the queen. We will meet her later."

Then Guinevere and Lancelot started to walk through the market together, Guinevere feeling surprisingly comfortable, but she didn't know if it was because of the disguise or because of Lancelot.

"You look like a knight," Guinevere finally asked. "Are you a knight?"

"What if I were to tell you that I am a great knight? Or what if I were a minor squire patrolling markets for maidens?"

Guinevere looked down at his sword and shield, noticing how clean they were, how they were free of spattered blood.

"A knight or a squire? May I choose which?"

Lancelot was further amused.

"Perhaps. And your are?"

"The queen, of course, in the market, accompanied by my servants. Or a fair maiden charmed by a minor squire. Perhaps."

"Perhaps charmed or perhaps a maiden?"

"Fair maiden," she said, correcting him.

"Oh, may I choose which kind of maiden?"

She smiled and looked down, and they walked on.

"May I ask you a question?" Guinevere said.

"You may ask me anything but a question?"

She smiled.

"Why did you give me a gift, present me with a flower?"

She had tucked the flower into a fold in her veil. Lancelot looked at it.

"Well, I saw you, a beautiful maiden, and felt the need to offer you flower. A simple gesture, I hope."

"I have never heard of a simple gesture."

"Aren't all gesture's simple?"

"And you felt you needed to?"

"To a lovely maiden, I felt I must."

"Must? So you felt obligated?"

"If you would like. Would you rather I didn't?"

"No, I was pleased."

"Well, good."

"I hope you don't mind me asking?"

"Not at all. And I'm sure there are a few more meanings to pluck from my gift."

Suddenly Guinevere had an idea.

"If you will excuse me a moment," she said. "I see a friend of mine, and I must ...very quickly."

Lancelot excused her, and she dashed away, disappearing around a tented shop. Lancelot didn't feel the least bit abandoned. Instead, he took the opportunity to exchange a few coins for a small basket of strawberries. Guinevere, however, was up to something else. She stopped behind the garment maker's shop, out of view, and whispered through the curtain. The proprietor appeared. Her words and soft gestures seemed to persuade him, and he handed her a wide swath of brown fabric, which she wrapped around her waist, and then she covered her head and shoulders with a wrinkled shall. Next, she politely took his cane.

Lancelot stood off to the side of the market foot traffic, nibbling slowly at the fruit, noticing how peaceful the crowd was, how content they seemed. He was looking the other way when he felt a tug on his shirt. He looked down and saw a hunched-over woman standing there. She leaned so heavily on her cane that it seemed the only thing keeping her from falling over. She put her hand out.

"A few coins for an old woman?" she said, her voice straining to enunciate her words.

Lancelot took notice of the softness of her hand, the dirt beneath her nails, and the smoothness of her skin.

"Ah, m'lady, surely." He took out his coin purse once more and placed a few gold pieces in her palm and smiled. "Whoops, I got some strawberry juice on the coins."

"That's OK. You are too generous."

"But don't tell anyone of my generosity. If people knew the size of my heart, it should be the end of me."

"You, sir, are a knight among men."

"M'lady, I am a knight among kings, but

nevertheless, I thank you for your kind words."

The old woman affected a subtle curtsy and took her leave. Lancelot turned the other way, partly to allow for her exit and partly to hide his smile. He ate another piece of fruit. A few moments passed, and Guinevere, from the opposite direction, came walking up.

"Did you miss me?" she asked, as if only one answer were possible.

"Strawberry?" He handed one to her, giving an extra glance at her palms.

"Thank you. Anything exciting happen while I was gone?"

"Nothing much."

He tried to maintain a straight face.

"Did I see you talking to an older woman?"

"Yes, just talking. Not that exciting, though."

Guinevere tried to figure out if his silence was in fact modesty. Lancelot ate some more fruit. They walked on. Lancelot, when Guinevere said something amusing, tested the boundaries and playfully bumped into her with his shoulder. Guinevere shouldered him back, but then looked down and away, wondering if she had crossed the line. The market stretched on, and they passed butchers and silk traders, more vegetable sellers and basket weavers. Children were circling a tented stall, what looked like a toy maker's shop. Lancelot saw kids playing out front, their mothers looking on. Guinevere spotted a jeweler's cart across the way.

"Let's look at some jewels." She asked.

"Just look?"

She smiled, and they walked over to the cart. The sun, from its angle in the sky, set the display cases ablaze with sparkles and shimmers. Guinevere scanned the arrangements, spotting, on a cushion of red velvet, a familiar white coil.

"Do you know what those are?" she asked.

"You mean the pearls?"

"How do you know? They are from the other side of the world and are new to England."

"I used to live in France."

"Oh?"

They both turned around. Guinevere was impressed but slightly bewildered by the man she was with, although bewildered in an appealing way. He seemed new and different, simple and unaffected. How easy his life must be, she thought, void of complications and of the demands she had always to contend herself with. And Lancelot, he knew exactly what his feelings were.

"May I surprise you with something?" he said.

"A surprise?"

Lancelot took out a strip of fabric and blindfolded Guinevere.

"Must be a special surprise," she said, and willfully submitted to the mystery.

"Now hold on. Stay here. Don't move."

Leaving Guinevere blind, he dashed in the jeweler's direction, but then circled back to the toy shop. From there he purchased a set of children's iron-cast marbles. Then he jogged back to the jewels, purchased the red velvet satchel, and then went back to Guinevere.

"Ok," he said. Holding the satchel behind his back, he removed the blindfold. "Now. I think there's something inside," he said with his sheepish smile. Lancelot placed the satchel in the palm of her hand.

"Why the blindfold?"

"If I couldn't wrap the gift itself...."

She inspected the outside of the satchel.

"I know this."

"Are you sure?"

She loosened the string, reached inside, and between her fingers rolled around its contents.

"From the jeweler's?"

"Keep going. Do it by feel," Lancelot slowly said, holding back the sly smile that Guinevere was beginning to figure out.

"The pearls?" she hesitatingly said. "But these are larger."

With her hand still in the bag, she whirled them around and around. Then her expression changed. She hadn't yet learned what Lancelot had already mastered, that of the noble gesture of letting a lie stand. When he saw the softness of the beggar woman's hand, he held his tongue. Guinevere was still discovering this temperament.

"I can feel the seams," she said.

Still smiling, "Whatever do you mean?"

"The seams. Pearls don't have seams."

She started to pull the contents out of the satchel, but then Lancelot quickly grabbed her hand.

"No. Why not keep the mystery? Let's do the ambiguous magnanimous gesture." Lancelot took the satchel from her, cinched it closed, and looked around. He spotted a mother and child walking by. He went up to her. Guinevere followed, blindfold off.

"Here." He handed her the velvet satchel. "But don't open it yet. Wait until we leave. It's a gift, for you."

"Or for your son," Guinevere chimed in.

"A gift for your son is also a gift for you, is it not? It's a gift either way."

The woman didn't know quite what to say, but accepted it and bowed politely. Lancelot and Guinevere stood there and watched them walk away.

"So, were they pearls?" Guinevere asked.

"We'll never know."

"You'll know."

"Perhaps, but a little mystery in our lives is good."

"Like whether you're a knight or a squire."

"Like whether you're the queen or a maiden."

She smiled for the first time the kind of smile

Lancelot had been offering her, a knowing smile.
"I'm sure we'll meet again...squire."
"I'm sure we will...fair maiden."

Chapter 8

The heels of Malagant's boots echoed in the corridors as he marched down the long hallway. A distant relative of King Arthur's, he had been one of the first knight's of the Round Table. But, through the exploration and conquering of other lands, new knights had been added to the select few of Arthur's inner circle. Malagant, though, had been around before the creation of the Round Table, and with all these new men, who were better swordsmen than he, better with the lance, more skilled at riding, and more loyal, more brave, and more respected, he had developed acute feelings of jealousy. And jealousy, over time, led to vindictiveness. He felt pushed aside, which had made him bitter, and as the wars had ended and the opportunities for questing had dried up, the chances for regaining favor with the king had withered as well. That's why this present summoning had him hurrying down the corridor. Arthur had sent word that he wanted to meet, and Malagant, like a neglected child, was eager to win back favor. He knocked on the big double doors to Arthur's chamber, and when he heard the word, "Enter," he quickly straightened his coat, brushed off his shoulders, and pushed the door open.

"Malagant, thank you for coming." Arthur was seated behind a large desk on top of which were various papers spread out. "I call on you because you have been with me since the old days. You know the kingdom well."

"Yes, my lord," he meekly answered.

"I've been going over my finances, the business reports, the taxes, and it looks like everything is in order. There are no more wars, nothing threatening on the horizon. But you might know. What is the next conflict?"

"Excuse me?"

"The next conflict, the next problem, the next issue, what will it be?"

Malagant was at a loss for words.

"You ask me, which I appreciate. And I have been with you since the beginning, that is true...."

"Can you answer the question?"

"My lord, the next issue...."

"Listen," Arthur said, "I will be getting a report on how the villagers feel. If all is fine, then we will know that all is not fine."

"I don't understand," Malagant said.

"Simple," Arthur said. "We know the villagers have complaints. That's what they do, complain. And if we don't hear them, then we aren't hearing them for a reason. And the reason is?" And when Malagant couldn't answer, "Because they are directed at me."

"At you?" Malagant said.

"Yes. For the villagers to complain is normal. Not to complain is abnormal, and therefore cause for alarm, cause for action. But we must figure out what," Arthur said. "For now, let's wait for the report from Guinevere. She is returning momentarily."

"You sent Guinevere to investigate? Is that safe?" Malagant said.

"She went in disguise. And I trust her. She should be back any moment, and she knows to come right to me. So, if she reports any negativity, we'll know everything is fine. But if she says anything positive, then all is wrong."

Just then, Guinevere pushed through the doors.

"Ah, my queen, you have news?"

Hearing the word "news," Guinevere couldn't help but smile, knowing that the real news was her interaction with the young man in the market.

"I do have news," she said, and then stopped when she saw Malagant.

"It's fine. You can speak in front of him," Arthur assured her.

"Yes, I do have news. The market couldn't be more thriving, and people couldn't be more content." She was glad to report such positive findings, and she delivered her news with a sing-song tone. "The merchants are doing very well, the sales are good, and the people were taking away carts full of produce, household wares, so we know they have money and are getting what they need."

"But did you hear any complaining?" Malagant interrupted.

Guinevere was taken aback.

"No. No complaining."

"There we have it," Arthur finished off, as if their earlier conclusions were now well established and final. Between the two men were anxious looks.

"Guinevere," Arthur said, "will you leave us? We have a meeting of the Round Table we must prepare for."

"Of course. But the news is good, right? All is good?"

"Thank you. Your news is integral. Now, if you'd let us prepare."

"Certainly," and she gave a slight curtsey and excused herself.

She was too preoccupied with thoughts of her own to concern herself with what they were up to. Instead, happy to be dismissed, she quickly, looking from room to room, almost prancing down the corridor, sought out Maerwynn, who she found in her chambers arranging her bottles.

"Maerwynn, Maerwynn, in the market today. That man...."

"You mean Sir Lancelot?" Maerwynn gave a guilty smile.

"Who?"

"Sir Lancelot," a voice said, coming from a chair off to the side. It was Victoria, lounging with a needle and thread, sewing a bit of lace onto the ruffles of a pillow. "Sir Lancelot, knight of the Round Table, the most accomplished, most decorated, most trusted knight in Camelot."

Guinevere looked at Maerwynn, who was nodding her head.

"Yes, she told me all about him when we parted."

"But I thought he was a squire." She sat back on a nearby chaise lounge to compose herself. "He said he was either a knight or a squire."

"Well, was he confident?" Maerwynn asked.

"Yes."

"Was he smart?" Victoria asked.

"And well spoken?" Maerwynn quickly added.

"Yes, he was."

"And, final question, was he handsome?" Maerwynn asked.

"Keep in mind we saw him, too," Victoria said, as if the answer were obvious.

"Victoria, I can't answer that with you here. I say one or two things about…"

"Lancelot," Maerwynn reminded her, with a giggle.

"…and it gets back to Arthur…"

"Your husband," Maerwynn interrupted again.

"I just…a compliment can be taken as more than a compliment, that's all."

Guinevere began to get nervous.

"Listen, Guinevere, my queen, my loyalty is to you. I was appointed to be your maiden, which also means that you have my complete confidence in all cases."

"But I am queen and he is a knight, and I am married to the king of Camelot."

"You can't help your feelings. You are responsible for your actions, not your feelings."

Maerwynn knew her sister well. Her intuition and

sensitivity told her things Guin could not even begin to realize.

"I have yet to confess any feelings," Guinevere insisted.

"You don't have to. When have you ever talked of any man like this?"

Victoria could only sit and listen to the sisters.

"Maerwynn, I haven't said more than twenty words."

"Look how you sit and fidget, and how defensive you are. I've been around you my whole life, and this is new. Didn't you once say something about what new feelings meant?"

Guinevere tried to force herself to sit still. She tried to look out the window, as if a distraction might come into view. "Oh, Victoria, I see you're sewing lace onto to a pillow." But that comment seemed forced and out of place, and even Victoria, for all her manners, didn't know how to respond. Maerwynn, letting her sister sit and fester in the most playfully antagonistic way, kept a subtle smile on her face, waiting for Guin to notice it. And when she did, Guin said:

"Maerwynn, what? I thought he was a squire."

"It makes no difference, does it?"

Chapter 9

Sir Lancelot strolled down the grand corridor toward the Great Hall, the meeting room for the Round Table. He shuffled his boots, ran his hand along the side ledges, and casually inspected the wall sconces whose torches lit the corridor. He was in no hurry. He was thinking about other things. From behind, a young knight ran up and clipped his shoulder.

"Lancelot, you need to be on guard."

It was Sir Lionel, his nephew, who had just been knighted and was over enthusiastic about being at the Round Table.

"Listen, Lionel, you're at this table today. If you don't show a little more respect, I can't hold your seat for you. Arthur will replace you."

"Oh Lancelot, you're always bringing me down. You should be happy."

"What do I have to be happy about?"

"What?"

"Go on. I'll see you in there."

Lionel skipped on ahead, "OK, but I'm sitting next to you."

Lancelot leaned against the wall, thinking about whether he was happy or not.

"What's this I heard? Nothing to be happy about?" It was Perceval. He leaned up against the wall, mimicking Lancelot's posture.

"Oh, Perceval. I met the queen to today."

"Guinevere?"

"Yeah. She tried to pretend she was a maiden."

"But you've never seen her before."

"I said I was either a knight or a squire. And then,

playing along, she said she was either the queen or a maiden. And no loyal subject of the queen would ever pretend to be the queen, even as a joke. So I knew it was her."

"And?"

Two knights walked passed them in the corridor, and they acknowledged each other with a nod.

"She tried to test my character by pretending to be a beggar."

"She did?"

"I think it was a test. But I could tell it was her. Her hands were clean. Underneath some dirty rags, her palms were spotless."

Strutting down the hall came Sir Gawain.

"Look at this boys, a new shiny belt. Extra shine means extra....We got to get to the meeting. Let's go."

And with that the three of the walked the rest of the way down the corridor, with Perceval looking over to Lancelot, trying to continue their conversation with a telling glances. But Lancelot just walked with his head down, deep in thought.

The Round Table had been installed in a large banquet hall, closed off to the rest of the castle proceedings. The chairs were all oaken high-backs whose lattice posts towered above its seat's occupant. And when the knights sat around the table, each, in front of them, had projected from the middle of the table inlaid leather with hobnail accents which fanned the table top, making it appear as though each of the twelve knights were at the head of the table. But when Arthur entered, all stood, waited for their king to be seated, and then sat back down.

"I've called this meeting to discuss some alarming findings," Arthur began, with Malagant seated at his side. He continued talking, but Lancelot was having trouble focusing, instead imagining where Guinevere was at this moment. She, however, was nearby, in a side chamber, peering out from behind a curtain at the Round Table. Maerwynn and Victoria were with her, huddling beside their queen, careful not to be seen.

"Now, which one is he?" Maerwynn asked with an excited giggle in her voice.

"There, on the side," Guinevere replied, and then, whispering under her breath, "So, he is a knight."

"The best knight," Victoria added, and Guin looked up at her and couldn't contain her girlish smile.

"What are they saying?" Guin said, struggling to hear.

"And so," Arthur continued, "the new policy, in the absence of war, will be to dispense justice." There was a grumbling from the knights. "You, as emissaries of peace and order, are to administer justice."

"But what does justice mean?" came from one from one of the knights.

"What does justice mean? As a member of the Round Table, if I have to explain what justice means to you, my most worthy and trusted knights, then we are lost."

Malagant leaned over and whispered something in Arthur's ear.

Guinevere turned to Victoria, "What does justice mean?" to which Victoria shook her head.

"If you'll excuse me for a moment," Arthur said, and stood up. "I shall return shortly." And he and Malagant left for his chamber.

Guinevere looked again and Victoria, who shrugged.

"We'll wait here," Maerwynn said. "See what happens."

Some of the knights stood up and talked among themselves.

"Well, boys, I have to go protect a farm," Gawain said, and he started to leave.

"You can't go yet," Perceval said.

"If Arthur can leave, so can I. The Round Table, we

are all equal."

Lancelot pushed back in his chair and went over to the hollow window cove behind them. Perceval, sensing tension, joined him.

"What's wrong?" he asked Lancelot.

"He is with her and I am not. So he is my enemy." His words were spoken as if he had no control over how he felt. "I don't wish him ill. I just wish him out of the way. And I don't feel bad about it."

"What are you talking about? You mean Guinevere?"

"We're not all equal at this Round Table."

"What are you talking about? And maybe we should keep our voices down."

Lancelot pulled Perceval further into the window cove. Guinevere peered around the curtain.

"What do you think they're talking about?" she whispered, referring to Lancelot and Perceval.

Other knights were talking of this and that, and their voices created a mix-matching of noises, but she could see the false squire and his friend across the room in the white light coming in from the window.

"About you. What else?" Maerwynn answered.

"Perceval, this table is false. No one is equal here."

"We are. No man is more than the next."

"You think Arthur believes himself a man?" Lancelot said, almost in disgust.

"They're probably saying how beautiful you are, how fair your skin is," Victoria said.

"No, Lancelot, we sit here, together, all of us equal at this table."

"But the power is not in the table. It's in the chairs." Perceval, in all his earnestness, tried to make sense of these words. Lancelot looked back to the leather and gold-gilded table. "Arthur poses as our equal, but how are we to forget he is king? How is he to forget?"

"Sssh, we should keep our voice down if we are to

say such things."

"And how lovely are your graces, your gestures," Maerwynn said.

"And how fine and silken you hair is," Victoria added.

Guin looked over at the two, careful to stay behind the curtain, "You really think so?"

"You set Arthur against us. But no, it is in the table. Look. It's round. It's circular. Against one another, there are no sides to take."

Lancelot had resigned himself to a quiet rage.

"A circle has but one side. And it's not ours."

"But he told us to do justice. Doing justice, how is that not a noble and egalitarian undertaking?"

"Justice? Tell me, what does that mean?" Perceval stood in silence. "It means the king's justice, his brand of justice. Don't you see that? He has given us a directive in which the only acceptable interpretation is to act in accordance with what the king wishes. There is no choice for us."

"But he is the king."

"Then he should just say so. We don't need these illusions of fairness."

Just then, King Arthur returned, with Malagant hurrying to stay at his side. The knights rushed to their seats, Lancelot somewhat begrudgingly, and Guinevere and her maidens turned their attention to the king.

"So, go forth and do justice," he continued. "Look carefully for those doing wrong. We have had some reports...."

"What reports?" a knight called out.

"Private reports. So be on the lookout. Now, this meeting is adjourned."

And with that the knights got up, somewhat puzzled, and began to exit. Lancelot, though, felt a hand on his shoulder, and when he turned around, Arthur stood there, with his broad shoulders square to the false squire.

"Sir Lancelot," he said, "have you had the pleasure of meeting your new queen? I don't believe I saw you at the wedding."

Lancelot looked at Perceval and then back to Arthur.

"The queen and I have not been formally introduced, correct."

"Well then, we should remedy that and meet her now." Arthur turned to a servant who was posted at the door behind where he had been seated. "Please find Queen Guinevere for me," and the servant pivoted and disappeared through the door.

When Guinevere heard this, she almost let out a cry, in part out of excitement and in part because she was away from her room. The three girls hurried away, bumping into each other, giggling. Victoria, playing the maternal role with her hand in the girls' backs, made sure they kept their balance while laughing and shuffling down the corridor. And while Maerwynn felt a welling up of a kind of lost adolescent enthusiasm, Guinevere noticed in herself, for the first time, some vague new feeling.

The girls got back to their room just as the servant came around the corner and then, pretending to be surprised and pleased that their presence was requested, followed him back to see Arthur. Lancelot, poised for the introduction, was standing in a dutiful pose next to Arthur, and when he saw Guin emerge apprehensively from the doorway, maintained his respectful disposition. Guin, however, seemed to tiptoe into the room, and her eyes were slow to look up from the floor.

"May I present Sir Lancelot, Knight of the Round Table. Lancelot, Guinevere, Queen of Camelot." Arthur's introduction was dwarfed by the nervous anxiousness there in the small antechamber beside the Grand Gallery. Victoria and Maerwynn tucked themselves on either side of the queen and quietly inspected the quiet knight. And then Lancelot stepped forward and went down on one knee.

"M'lady," he quietly said, as he took her hand in his and brought it up to his lips as if for a kiss, but he paused just short of his lips, and then released her hand. Never had so simple a gesture carried so much weight. Arthur was the first to speak up after this introduction.

"Lancelot," he said, turning to Guin, "was unable to attend our wedding."

"Is that true?" Guin asked without a hint of consternation.

"I'm afraid so."

"And the reason is?" she continued.

"I'm sure no reason I give will suffice, but if there were a way I could win back your good graces...."

"There is," Maerwynn interrupted. "Your Majesty," she directed at Arthur, "the three of us were earlier remarking that our horse-riding skills could use some polishing. And as it wouldn't be prudent for us to go galloping about on our own outside the walls, would it not be good penance for Lancelot to chaperon us, perhaps even teach us the finer points of riding?"

There was a silence while Arthur pondered the idea. Guin, without drawing attention to herself, reached back behind her and grabbed her sister's hand in anticipation. But then Victoria spoke.

"Although perhaps it would just be you two. I have a previous engagement I really must attend to."

Arthur nodded.

"Then it's settled." In his good-natured way, "Lancelot, I order you to chaperon them on a riding expedition."

"An expedition, Sir?"

The mood was suddenly lighter.

"Yes. You are to see if you can, in this land of mine, discover if there is any fun to be had."

"An expedition for fun?" Maerwynn played the game.

"Of course." Turing to his knight, "Although the matter is settled and there's really no way of getting out of it, let me ask you: Would you be happy to go on an expedition of fun?"

"Normally, as a knight, I would never confuse fun with happiness. So, if you'll permit me," he said breaking into a smile, "I would rather consider this my penance as Maerwynn suggested."

"Very well then," Arthur said, as he spotted Malagant walk by in the hall. Suddenly his expression changed, and he started to excuse himself. "Early, then, tomorrow. Now, I have some matters to take care of," and he quickly followed after Malagant in the hall. Guinevere, Maerwynn, and Victoria were left alone in the small antechamber with Lancelot. The well-traveled and much-experienced knight stood there calmly, while the three girls, all somewhat in shock, mildly panicked in silence, until Lancelot said dryly:

"Thank you. Now I'm going to have to go teach myself how to ride."

The girls all looked at each other.

"But I thought you were a knight?" Maerwynn said. "Don't you know how to ride a horse?"

Lancelot didn't break expression.

"I mean teach myself to ride badly, so you can keep up."

Their smiles widened. Guinevere turned her back to Lancelot, to face Maerwynn and Victoria, and raised her eyebrows and gave a nod to indicate they should leave her to their riding instructor. Maerwynn picked up on it immediately and took Victoria by the arm to escort her away.

"You really have something else to do?" Maerwynn asked Victoria when they were out of earshot.

"Now Guin has one less person as a distraction."

"Wait. You mean I'm a distraction?"

The two girls walked on. Guin turned to face Lancelot there in the small antechamber, knowing they couldn't remain isolated like that for long.

"Riding lessons?" Lancelot said.

"She made that up."

"You would give your sister away like that to me? That tells me something."

"I think she'd be fine with that."

"No, not about how you treat your sister. Giving her up tells me something about how you feel about me."

Guin, her feelings exposed, didn't pursue the topic further.

"So you're a knight and not a squire?"

"Was there ever any question?"

"Well..."

"But you know I knew you were the queen all along."

"How?"

"Your clean white hands."

"Really?"

"Do you still have the coins I gave you?"

"How did you know that was me in disguise?" She thought for a moment. "Oh, my clean white hands, right." And they both nodded in unison. She composed herself. "We probably shouldn't be caught here alone."

"Why? Are you nervous?"

Lancelot knew what he was doing.

"No," she said, as if that was a ridiculous suggestion.

But then Lancelot took a step forward, so that they were mere inches apart. Guin froze.

"Are you nervous now?" he said.

But then Lancelot returned to his respectable distance, and they each sensed it was time to part.

"My Queen, are you sure riding lessons are a good idea if there will be issues."

As this was the final chance for her to assert herself, she summoned up her courage.

"Oh, there will be issues," she said. "I'm sure of it. And I'm also sure lessons are a good idea."

Chapter 10

The next morning Guinevere and Maerwynn, in their riding gear, were waiting out by the King's stables when Lancelot came galloping up from over the bluff. He dismounted and tied his horse up at the post.

"Oh, you have a beautiful horse," Maerwynn said, running her hand down its mane. "What's his name?"

"I see you noticed it was a him," Lancelot said and smiled.

"Him is the default preposition. I study language."

Her tone had an air of superiority.

"Well, he doesn't have a name, and if you study language, then you'll know why."

"You haven't named your horse," Guin said. "Why not?"

"Because I would never ask of him what I wouldn't ask of myself."

"But you have a name?" Guin persisted.

"Why don't you two get your horses, and we can talk about it on the way."

"On the way to where?" Maerwynn said.

A stable boy brought around two sturdy-looking steeds, and the girls easily mounted them.

"Not dresses but riding pants? No sidesaddle for you two?"

"Our father taught us how to ride," Guin said.

"On the way to where?" Maerwynn repeated.

"To fun. Isn't that what the king said?"

And with that the two girls snapped the reins and their horses jerked forward to a moderate trot. Lancelot, understanding they were now in his care, patted his sword at his side and jabbed his heal into his horse. The girls were soon galloping up the slope of the bluff, and Lancelot, knowing his horse's speed, veered off to the right to outflank the sisters. He, without hesitating, split the high grasses, leaped over a felled tree, and splashed through a creek, all the while keeping the girls in view as he passed them by. Guin and Maerwynn soon had had enough of the charade. There was no race. So they pulled up and came to halt. They circled their horses around to look for Lancelot.

"Where is he?" Maerwynn said.

Guin smiled, and without looking said, "He is behind us," and she brought her horse back around. And there was Lancelot, leaning forward with his hands crossed over the pommel of his saddle.

"I guess we found it," Lancelot said.

"What?" said Guin.

"Fun," said Maerwynn.

"But I think there's some more over there," the knight said, motioning further up ahead. "But let's ride slower. We'll cover more ground."

The three of them rode on, side-by-side, with Lancelot in the middle. The morning dew was still on the ground, and the fields of lilac on the upslope of the adjacent knoll made it seem as if an avalanche of purple had frozen in place. The trees were sparse now, and the rolling brown grasses colored the landscape in patches of various tans and auburns. All was quiet save for the lonely chirp of a bird and the breeze waving through the lilac stalks.

"So, really, why don't you name your horse?" Guin said.

"Do you know what it means to be a knight of the Round Table?"

"I've noticed that you have no set coat of armor, no uniform shields or helmets," Maerwynn said.

Lancelot, as he was in the middle, turned to face her.

"Do you know why that is? Because we take our boots, our swords and shields, all of it, off those we kill."

"You do?" Guin said, and Lancelot turned to her.

"Yes. That is why we all look different."

"So," Maerwynn started in. She recognized, because the knight was in the middle, that talking meant his full attention to the exclusion of her sister. "So, then going on quests, fighting, killing, they are just means of going shopping?"

"I know a knight who just wanted a new shiny belt."

"And that meant killing someone for it?" Guin said, almost in horror.

"Well, I'm sure he just picked that up in the market."

"But you, too? What you're wearing was once worn by a man you killed?"

"I am a knight." But Lancelot could see this was upsetting the queen, so he tried to lighten the mood. "Me, however, it was tough. I was always sent off to slay giants and phantoms. The giants' armor was too big, and the phantoms, well, you could imagine." Maerwynn let out boisterous laugh, and Guin, recognizing Lancelot's change of tone, let her eyes smile for her. "And the dragons," he continued, "well...."

"I heard," Maerwynn said, "that a knight once cut off a dragon's wings and tried to use them himself to fly. It's just what I heard."

Lancelot shook his head, and then plainly said, "You know dragons don't actually exist."

"What? But I heard...."

"It's all made up. There are no dragons. It's just to impress people, to create heroes, to make the townspeople trust those who are supposed to protect them. I'm not supposed to tell anyone, but you're royalty, so...."

"But the phantoms are real?" Maerwynn sarcastically said.

"Please, I've said too much," he said, trying to let the ambiguity stand.

"You'd betray your fellow knights to us?" Guin quietly said, leaning in. "That tells me something."

Lancelot looked into her eyes.

"It should."

"But then you are a bunch of frauds." Maerwynn's objection broke up the moment. "It's all for show. What heroes?" she said under her breath.

"Respectfully, M'lady," he said to Maerwynn. "These heroes saved your father's kingdom, and maybe even saved your lives."

"But then why lie? To impress us naïve maidens?"

"Well, yes. When the king was putting his collection of knights together, he had to raise taxes in order to get enough money to entice the best men from all over the country to join him. But the people objected, and to convince them that knights were needed, we had to show them that ominous threats existed. So you see, it was a lie that saved your kingdom."

Maerwynn was quiet. They rode on, through a small grove of trees, until they came to a creek.

"Here," Lancelot said and dismounted. "Let's let the horses rest a while. We'll tie them up here on these branches and this will give them enough slack to drink from the creek."

The girls hopped off and tied their horses up next to the knight's, although Guin seemed to have trouble securing her straps to the branch.

"For someone who refuses to name his horse, you sure treat it well," Guin said.

"Yes, you never fully answered our question. Why can't you just make up a name?" Maerwynn added.

The three off them slowly walked toward a shady spot.

"It's a long story."

"We have time," Guin said.

"Oh, do we?" Lancelot smiled. "All right. I treat him well so he performs for me, and I don't name him so I can ride him into the ground and then abandon or kill him without compunction."

The girls stopped. They were shocked.

"But you said you would never ask of your horse what you wouldn't ask of yourself," Guin said.

"That's right. Here, do you mind if we sit?" The three of them sat down beneath a large elm tree. When Guin saw Lancelot lie on his back, she, too, reclined in the grass, and Maerwynn followed. Lancelot continued with his explanation while looking up at the sky. "I spent a lot of time in the East, all around really, and there I learned how to systematically die, to kill myself at the beginning of each day so that I may get the courage from living on, undead. Eh, but let's talk about something else. Did you see the sunrise this morning?" Lancelot laughed. "I'm joking."

Guinevere reached over and playfully slapped him on the chest. Maerwynn saw this.

"OK. Let's talk about love," she said.

"Right. Let's not talk about anything serious," Lancelot said, and looked over at Guin.

Maerwynn went on talking. "The other day I was doing an assignment for my tutor, and I had to come up with metaphors for love. Having been "all around," as you say, how would you describe love?"

"Sure. Love." Lancelot thought for a moment. "Well, if you're a student of language, then you know love is the source of all evil." Guinevere, remembering her wedding day, looked at Lancelot out of the corned of her eye. He continued: "But let's not pretend we're going to come up with anything new on a subject that everyone thinks about all the time."

"It doesn't have to be new," Maerwynn said, "just

what do you think?"

"Let's talk about it this way. I saw the devastation of the lands of your father's kingdom, I was there. What do you think about that? What should be done with the toppled and burnt forests, the ruined villages?"

"You're asking us?" Guin said, unsure where he was going.

"We should rebuild," Maerwynn said with certainty. "Repair the villages, replant the forests. What was there before should be there again."

"I think, and I hate to put it too coldly, that we should just get on with our lives," Guin said.

"People need places to live, sure, but build new villages. The forest will regenerate itself. Let's look forward, not try to recapture what was lost."

"But Guin," her sister objected, "houses that have been in families for generations, how do you throw that entire heritage away? And nature, why wouldn't we want her to be at her best? Which of us would want to be burned and devastated and just abandoned?"

"Nothing was lost in the war that wasn't already lost to begin with," Lancelot said abruptly. "Guinevere is right, though." And he blindly reached over to Guin, and she watched his hand touch her forearm. "The first lesson of war, or of life for that matter, is to realize that everything is already lost, for we always fight the hardest for what we know is hopeless. And that mourning must be a forward action. And Maerwynn, you talk about nature as a "her," and I realize that's a default preposition. But why is it a her instead of an it? And why think that nature has a "best?" It doesn't. Why do you give nature human characteristics it does not otherwise possess?" Lancelot turned over to lie on his stomach. "I said I would only demand of my horse what I would be prepared to sacrifice myself. And as my horse may perish, so may I, but I do so serving the needs of man...or woman. Not trees. Not villages. Not the wind-swept grass. I fight for people. And so when we endow nature with human qualities, why do we do that? It's not to relate to it or to better understand it. We call it a her to give it the human capacity to love, so that it might love us. You want to know about love? That's what we are always searching for, someone or something to love us. But, to take Guin's point, the only way to live is to realize that love is already lost." The girls were silent. "Maybe we should get back to the castle."

They stood up in silence and brushed the grass from their clothes. Walking back to the horses, Maerwynn noticed one was missing. It was Guinevere's.

"Guin, your horse, it's gone."

"What?" she said with an odd tone. "Well, I guess," she said slowly, "that I might have to ride with you, Lancelot."

Maerwynn mounted her horse. Lancelot, atop his unnamed steed, reached out, gripped Guin under her arm, and in one motion pulled her up to ride behind him. Guin couldn't conceal her smile, and wrapped her arms around his waist. Maerwynn brought her horse around and leaned over to whisper into her sister's ear.

"See? Nothing is lost."

And with that they galloped back to the castle.

Chapter 11

Victoria stood out on the balcony, which overlooked the western castle wall. The patches of farmland checkered the countryside, and she gazed among the distant trees, to the carts rolling over the narrow bridge that traversed a neighboring creek, to the peasants in the king's garden who were raking and watering the soil.

"You don't think it's too much, do you?"

Arthur had strolled up behind her to join her on the balcony.

"What is too much?"

"All this."

"How do you mean?"

"How am I to provide for all them? More land, more livestock, more grain, more vegetables, more wood for pens and fences and huts. Where will it come from?"

Victoria was at a loss for words. They both continued to scan the land below as if the answer was out there among the fields.

"Sire, I do not—"

"Victoria, I appointed you special maiden to Guinevere because I trusted that you would act in her best interest. You're counseling her well, aren't you?"

"I believe so."

Arthur, entertaining two thoughts, moved between conversations.

"Without wars or quests for the knights, what do the people latch onto?"

"Sire? Are you all right?"

Arthur was quiet, staring off into the distance.

Then his eyes moved up into the clouds, which coated the sky in grays and whites.

"The heavens, do they move independently of the earth?"

Victoria saw Arthur's head tilted back and matched his view. She looked at the clouds as if they were new to her, mysterious and new, and followed the silver outlines of the tufts from cloud to cloud.

"And the farmland. Look." And they both lowered their chins again to the Earth. "To call the squares of crops a quilt is hardly original. We've heard that before. But the sky and the land, each separate and flowing. What unites them? Now, look here." Arthur turned around, as did Victoria, and looked above them, up at the spire atop the roof of the tower. Clouds slowly drifted past, so close the weather vane seemed to drag through and tear them. "Like a quit, where a point connects two pieces of fabric and holds them in place—here, I unite the land and the heavens." Arthur then, for the first time, looked directly at Victoria. "Do you see the difference?"

Arthur was deep in his reverie, and, as Victoria sensed, no part of his body seemed to make any connection with the balcony, not his boots, not his coat with the air around him, and not the face into which Victoria searched for a hint as to the correct response.

"The difference?" she said.

"Between the Earth and the World."

"Sire?"

Arthur looked down and saw horses galloping diagonally across the fields. Maerwynn and Lancelot with Guinevere were returning. Arthur continued his thought.

"The Earth is the Earth, but with Guinevere in it, the Earth becomes the World." He paused. "Now go," the king went on, "and welcome the queen home."

Victoria curtsied and quickly disappeared into the tower. Arthur leaned over the railing to get a closer view and saw clearly now that there were only two horses, and he saw who was on them. Victoria hurried down the stairs, down a hallway, past the kitchen where the royal chefs were already preparing dinner, down another hallway, along a colonnade lining an open-air atrium, and met Guinevere and Maerwynn coming in through the double doors.

"How was it?" she said, out of breath.

The girls could barely contain themselves, and Guin looked around for an out-of-the-way place to pull Victoria into. But the curtains were too shallow, and a servant was approaching, and some voices were carrying in from a nearby chamber.

"To my room," she said, taking Victoria by the wrist.

"No, not here," Maerwynn interrupted, fearing Arthur may walk in. "To my room."

And the girls ran down the hall, trying to contain their giggles. But Arthur was proceeding down an adjacent passage, and he could hear their faint laughter caroming off the stone walls. Once he identified it, he tried to ignore the sounds, but his mind kept returning to it. And how foreign it was to him, how he knew the giggles stemmed from an attitude that was long ago dampened by the quilt of his kingdom.

The girls burst into Maerwynn's chamber, and Guin closed the door behind them.

"So what happened, what happened?" Victoria said.

They all fell upon the bed, and the colored glass from the bottles filtered the torch light, spreading over them the broad beams of cherry red, emerald green, and a soft honeyed glow. Guin lay on her back and stared up at the ceiling.

"I don't know what to say."

"No, come on. Tell me all about it," Victoria said, hopping up to her knees.

And then Guin rolled over.

"But what now?"

"What do you mean 'what now?'" Maerwynn said, and she rolled over to copy her sister's posture.

"We went for a ride, and it seemed to go by so quickly. Where do we go from here? And I'm not even sure what we're doing?"

"Do you want to see him again tonight?" Victoria said. She had this secret bit of information and was waiting on the balcony so she could run tell Guin right away.

"Tonight?"

"At Ryerson Hall. All the knights congregate there, drinking. He'll be there tonight."

"But so what if he's there?" Maerwynn said, but Guin and Victoria only seemed to have tunnel vision for each other.

"Ryerson Hall? What am I supposed to do?"

"Your Highness," Victoria said, adopting a professional tone, "Perhaps you should go in disguise again to gather further details about the mood of the townspeople?"

"But what would I wear?"

Victoria got off the bed and went to the closet.

"Maerwynn, you have plenty of stuff," and she started pulling out different dresses and shawls and shoes, while Maerwynn sat on the bed and tried to figure out how to object.

"But, but, it'll be night time. You can't go out."

"You heard. It's for research," Victoria said, and it was the first time Maerwynn felt their servant taking sides.

"Maerwynn, it'll be fine. It's a beer hall," Guin said.

"I hope you know what you're doing." And with that Maerwynn fell back on the bed and enclosed herself in honey-colored light.

Chapter 12

Ryerson Pub was located at the far end of the market. It was one of the few large structures the villagers outside the walls had to themselves, and so it doubled as both a brew hall and a meeting place for the people. Arthur had allowed its construction, although it was financed and built by a group of local businessmen, including the proprietor of the fish market and a collection of the successful hunters as a place to sell the animals they trapped and killed. The hall was made from a circle of enormous tree trunks planted vertically in the ground and then cross-stacked with horizontal logs to make the hall look like a fortress rather than like one of the flimsy barns that housed hay and grain for the livestock. The dirt that surrounded the hall was worn into a series of matted-down tracks that led straight to the entryway, and the torchlight from the hall made the place seem like one of the peasant's smoldering bread ovens.

"And I said, 'If it must needs be.'"

Lancelot and Perceval were seated at one of the long tables, a ways down from the other men.

"You said needs must what?" Lancelot asked. He didn't quite get the order of the words.

"If it must needs be. It's from Hector of Errendoq. I was on a quest to kill him, and then when I had my sword to his throat and he was begging for mercy, he suddenly became quiet, and then said, 'If it must needs be.'"

"If it must needs be. That's an interesting way to put it. If it must needs be. And then you sliced him?"

"And then I let him go. I was so turned around by the phrase, if it must needs be, that I granted his mercy."

"Oh. The phrase is so fun to say, you should have lived up to it."

"I know. He came after me two days later, and I had to fight him in a stream and my boots got soaked through."

"But...If it must needs be?"

"If it must needs be. Fate was served. He soon floated down the river, face down."

They each took a drink of their beers from giant steins. Other knights were at the various tables and in the corners talking to each other and making remarks to the waitresses and the women passing by in their flouncy dresses. But it wasn't about unwinding and relieving stress from busy days of sword-wielding and foe-vanquishing, for there was actually nothing of any importance for the knights to do. The directive from Arthur about "doing justice" was so vague, the knights, not just of the Round Table but all of them, had let the king's words fall by the wayside. And so their talk was of the old days, of trying to keep alive the stories of their daring heroics. But Lancelot and Perceval were talking of something else.

"So, Lance, when she was on the back of your horse, what did you say? What did she say?"

But before Lancelot could answer, Gawain came over with a round of fresh beers.

"We need to have more beers on the table. Women will see this, know we're out to have a good time, and then want to join us."

"And that on your shoulders. They're new?" Lancelot said.

Gawain had new pauldrons, shining in the flickering firelight, affixed to his shoulders, making his frame seem broader.

"Brand new. In profile," he said, turning sideways to demonstrate, "they give my stature more prominence, don't you think?" And just then, looking toward the bar, he spotted a woman eyeing him, and he nodded, and then sat down with the two knights. "It's just that easy."

"Don't those impede your motion when you swing your sword?" Perceval said.

"Come on. Those days are over. I mean, Lancelot, do you still even sharpen your sword?"

"After every time I use it?"

"Yes, and when was that?"

"Today."

"What did you use it on?"

"The air."

Gawain laughed.

"You think fighting against shadows dulls your sword?" Lancelot smiled and looked around the room, and on one of the back benches he saw a curiously dressed woman. In the dim light, her white and yellow dress made her seem out of place. She had scooted over next to a knight who had a woman sitting on his lap, and Lancelot was certain this mysterious woman was alone. Gawain continued, "Oh, Lancelot, if you're reduced to trying to slay the mist, what will you do when you meet with some real resistance? What you need is a quest."

Lancelot got up to go approach the woman.

"The sharper the sword, the easier it cuts, and the less work your shoulders do," he said almost absentmindedly, not taking his eyes off the woman.

He made his way around a table of loud boisterous knights and past a man slouched over with his head down next to his beer stein, never taking his eyes off the woman in yellow and white. As he got closer, he saw she had thick black hair, and then he unleashed a wide grin. The woman saw him coming nearer, and she tried to avert her gaze and pretend she was occupied by some small task.

"Is that black hair supposed to fool me?" he said.

"It is supposed to fool everyone but you," Guinevere said.

"Are you here by chance?"

"What do you think?" she said.

Lancelot reached out and gently grabbed her hand.

"What?" she said.

"You're going to come sit with us."

"But only for a short while."

"For however long you want," Lancelot said, and he led her across the hall and back to his table. But when he arrived, sitting in his spot was Sir Kay, and Guin recognized him at once.

"Ah, Lancelot," Kay said. "You don't normally come in here. What, had enough of lying in the fields? Is she from the fields, as well?" Sir Kay extended his hand to Guin. "I don't believe we've met. I am Sir Kay, knight of the Round Table."

"How come you always say that you're part of the Round Table?" Perceval asked.

"It's a distinction. I've earned it. Unlike those shoulder pieces on you, Gawain."

Lancelot and Guin sat down side-by-side next to Perceval, with Gawain and Kay on the other side of the table. A peasant woman, half drunken, had seated herself next to Gawain on the end bench.

"What earned?" Gawain said in mock objection. "These," referring to the shining metal, "are the new currency."

"Is that right?" Kay continued, and then motioned to the woman at the end of the table. "Nice purchase."

"You can't talk about her like that," Guin said.

Sir Kay was taken aback by her outburst.

"I'm a knight, seneschal to the king. I say as I please?"

"Let's not," Lancelot said.

"Perhaps if you had put more beers on the table," Gawain said, "this young woman might have fallen in line." Gawain winked at Guin, who smiled back, seeing it was a joke.

"Incidentally, I know a girl," Guin said to Gawain, "who is infinitely charmed by colored glass."

"Oh, do you?" Gawain said.

"Who is it?" Kay said. "Is it the queen, and is the colored glass cut and placed in metal casings to fit on her fingers and to dangle around her neck and to wear atop her head?"

Guin sat still, and Lancelot moved forward on the bench.

"Yes," Lancelot said to Guin, "Is it the queen?" He smiled and nudged her under the table.

Certainly Guin was talking about her sister's bottle collection, but Kay's comment left her more in the mood to continue the awkward moment than to take offence. Growing up a princess and hearing her fair share of insults, she had developed a thick skin.

"I'm sorry," she began, "you said you were Sir Kay, a knight of the Round Table?"

"That's right," Kay said, "and seneschal to the king."

"And as a knight, you've been on many quests?"

"Of course."

There was a basket of bread in the center of the table, and Gawain pulled the basket toward him and offered one to Perceval, who took one and over-pronounced his gratitude, and Gawain affected a humble bow.

"And you've slain many villains?" Guin spoke with a soft patronizing tone.

He nodded.

"I am impressed," she said. "You must have courage and valor and strength."

Lancelot nudged her again under the table, but this time trying to signal her to take it easy.

"I said I was a knight," Kay said, as if the word knight was synonymous with all superlative traits.

"I have even heard the most fabulous tales of

knights slaying dragons. Surely, that must take the most courage of all. Sir Kay, knight of the Round Table, how many dragons have you slain?"

She leaned in with her elbows on the table and rested her chin in her palms, awaiting his answer.

And very calmly, Kay said, "Eight."

"Wow," Guin said.

Sir Kay was proud of his announcement. Lancelot sat back and looked around the room at other women fawning over other knights, emptying beer steins with one hand while the other was wrapped around the dirty necks of men whose gallantry was growing increasingly obsolete.

"And you, my good lady," Gawain said, tearing off a bit of his bread and eating it with a mischievous grin, "well done. With sorcery like that, you must be some kind of witch."

Guin plucked one of the small loaves of bread the size of her fist from the basket. "The kind of witch who can take a loaf as hard as a rock," she said as she reached under the table and wrapped on the wood as she pretended to knock on the table top with the loaf, making it seem as if the loaf were hard as a rock and making the thud. "And can then make it bounce." With the bread in her hand, she acted as though she were throwing it down to have it bounce off the ground. But she let her throwing hand continue past the lip of the table so Kay and Gawain on the other side couldn't see her then turn her wrist over, bread still in hand, stomp the ground with her foot, and then flip the bread up into the air. Gawain and Kay heard the stomp and saw the bread fly up past the lip and above their heads.

"Surely, a witch," Gawain laughed and patted Kay on the back, but Kay just sat there, silent.

Guin stood up.

"Lancelot, is it? Would you use your courage to walk me home?" And without waiting for his answer, she turned and made her way to the door.

"M'lady calls," Lancelot said, and then caught the eye of Perceval. "If it must needs be."

Perceval then stretched out and tapped Gawain on his shoulder plate. Gawain raised his eyebrows to Perceval and nodded over to the half-drunken woman at the end of the table who hadn't said a word all evening.

But someone was looking on from the corner. Although the conversation was lost on him, he saw the exchange, saw the glances, squinted to see the nudges under the table, and saw the two leave together. Drink in his hand, he lifted it to his lips, and then went on with words to his tablemates. It was Malagant. When Guinevere and Lancelot got outside, immediately Guin said, "We had a court jester when I was growing up."

A breeze was blowing, and the trees that crowded the road in front of the hall channeled it, and the breeze blew the hair of Guin's wig forward and into her face as she and Lancelot walked. They didn't speak for a few moments. Guin saw the ruts in the road and tried to inspect how they were formed and how they moved off into the distance.

"Lance, the ground by my father's castle is so trampled that it runs smooth, like the floor in the hall. But theses ruts...."

He interrupted her.

"Guin, you are an expert rider, and there is no way you would not tie your horse up correctly."

"Fair enough."

"And there is no way you would appear at the hall by chance."

The breeze whipped at her hair, and she had to walk facing Lancelot to keep it out of her eyes.

"I'm on a mission to collect information about the state of things."

Lancelot tilted his brow forward.

"Is that the explanation for me, or is that what you told Arthur?"

She stayed silent, but then changed the subject.

"Sir Gawain's metal shoulder things, what is that about?"

"Oh. He thinks they will signal to women that he is fit to be pursued."

"Fit to be pursued? The shiny metal is communicating that?"

"Right."

"What woman would fall for something like that?"

"I know," Lancelot agreed.

"I mean, only a desperate, uneducated fool."

"Well, Guin, what can I tell you? If it must needs be."

But Guin continued her disgust and mocked how the seduction must happen.

"Ooh, look, shiny on his shoulders." She put her hands up to feign praise. "Surely, he must be the one. What a joke."

"We call them japes."

"What do you mean?"

"A joke, us knights, we call them japes."

"Well that shoulder metal, surely it is a jape."

"We will see."

As they walked further into the blackness, Guin's stride became a kind of stroll, and Lancelot read into that stroll a certain attitude.

"You seem comfortable not playing the queen."

She wound her finger through the strands of her black wig.

"I suppose. That's funny, isn't it? I'm more comfortable in costume than when I'm playing me."

"Sure. You play you, but are the disguise," Lancelot said, brushing a branch aside that hung down in their path.

"And you, Lancelot, you play a knight or are a knight?"

"Both, I guess. You know how it goes. Am I brave because I just am brave, or am I brave because I want to be brave so I act brave and, in acting, I am."

"What did you say about talking about love? We're not going to come up with anything that hasn't been said before, so why try?"

"Something like that, but that was then."

"Oh, it is different now?" she said and smiled.

"I don't speak to universals. I speak for myself, how I feel."

"Ah, my arm," Guin called out. As Lancelot was finishing his sentence, Guin had walked into a low-hanging branch, and a thorn had pierced her forearm, drawing a small trickle of blood. Droplets fell on her dress. "The branch, it got me on the arm."

"Here, let me see," Lancelot said, reaching for her arm, but she pulled away.

"I can do it. It's just a scratch. It's nothing."

"I just want to see, that's all."

"Because I'm fine. I am."

She thought Lancelot was thinking he was going to fix everything.

"I know you are fine." He took her arm. "It's only a red dot."

"See. I'm fine."

They played at reassuring each other.

"I know you are."

"Just fine."

"Because you're Guin, the queen."

"Guin?"

"Oh. Is it acceptable to call you that?"

"It's a little familiar, don't you think?"

"So you can have your arms around me on the back of the horse, but I can't call you by your name?"

Lancelot wasn't seriously objecting, only instigating a little harmless confrontation. But she ignored his question. Instead, she inspected her dress.

"These red dots, they're not going to come out."

"You're the queen. You throw the dress away and get a new one."

"Not me. Others might thinks it's ruined, but I'm the kind of person who'll work at it, try to fix it. And I know it will set by the time I get back, and that it will probably be permanent. But, you know, that's just how I am. And part of me has to work on it just because I know it likely won't come out. Hopeless, perhaps, but I must try?"

"Not me. If something is ruined, I get a new one. Like my horse, and with all due respect, he is a tool to be used. If my tools are less than perfect, I cannot have that, because they cannot fail me when I need them the most.

"So I will fight for a dress, and you will give up on your horse? Does that sound right? And you, don't you literally fight for your clothes, taking what you have off the people you kill?"

"Well, I am talking about my professional conduct, and you are talking about some pieces of fabric."

A slow smile formed on Guin's face.

"Sir Gawain wouldn't call them pieces of fabric."

Lancelot also moved to keep the mood light.

"And you talk about the red dots being permanent. But if you can make bread solid as a rock bounce off the ground, maybe you really can get that blood out."

"Because, after all, I'm a witch, remember?"

"Right, he called you a witch."

"So I'm either a queen or a maiden or a witch."

"If it needs must be," Lancelot said, as the breeze blew leaves across the darkened path.

Chapter 13

The morning mist had already burned off, and the sun was intensifying the golden colors of the wheat fields. The rolling hills that swept down from the plateaus curled the wheat stalks in and out of valleys, and as the fields lead down to the road, the splayed branches of a great twisted oak tree offered a patch of shade. And with the hills growing increasing grayer as they were layered in the distance, and with the golden wheat surrounding the oak tree like an encroaching fire, Lancelot lay asleep. He had put his shield beside his head, anticipating the shifting sunlight and ensuring shade for himself into the afternoon. But soon, the lulling sound of shushing wheat stalks was interrupted by the melodic clomping of an approaching horse. Lancelot squinted to make out the galloping figure, but the image was obscured in the blinding sunlight. And then he heard his name being called out, and instantly he recognized Perceval's voice. Slowly, he rolled over onto his side as Perceval dismounted.

"Sorry to wake you," Perceval said.

"If anyone, I'm glad it's you."

"And it would have to be me, because I was the only one who knew where to find you."

"So you came on purpose to get me?"

"On purpose, yes, I was ordered."

Lancelot was quiet, as this was too much for him, just having woken up.

"All right, what's the order?" he said.

"You are to come back with me. A trade emissary from one of the continental kingdoms has arrived, and they're going on a picnic or something. We are to provide security."

"Why can't Arthur use his usual guards? Why us knights?"

"I don't know. Because we're knights and he's trying to impress them."

Lancelot got up, secured his shield and sword to his side, grabbed Perceval's extended hand, and mounted the horse behind his friend.

"Them? Who's the them again?" Lancelot asked.

"A trade emissary. That's all I know."

They started to trot back to the castle.

"Putting us on duty, what are they looking to trade?" Lancelot said and shook his head.

King Arthur and Sir Malagant were standing in a small side chamber away from the rest of the waiting receiving party.

"Now, Malagant," Arthur said in a hushed voice, "your job is to keep people away from us. If this is going to work, it has to come down to a he said-she said, so there cannot be corroborating witnesses. Princess Adelina, she thinks she is here on a trade mission, but I will really be trying to provoke a war. But it will be subtle, because I need honest grounds to say that she instigated it."

"But what about her protector, Sir Sebastian?"

"He will ride on top of the carriage. And I have selected a place for lunch that we will not get to very quickly, so that will give me plenty of time with her alone."

"Alone? In the carriage, there is room for four, maybe even six?" Malagant said.

"For comfort's sake, we will do four."

"But which four?"

"Me, Guinevere, The Princess, and you?"

"Not me. Might I suggest someone else? I have sent for Lancelot. Perhaps he could be the fourth?"

Arthur paused.

"You sent for him?"

"I was just going to have him attend, but if he is the fourth, think about it, Your Highness. He is honest, yes, and everyone knows. But even more, he is loyal. And so he will back your side of the provocation, and his known integrity will make it convincing. So he should be the fourth."

"Yes. His integrity is beyond reproach."

There was a knock at the door. Malagant opened it, and a servant stepped in.

"Sir Malagant, Sir Perceval is back."

"And?"

"He has him."

"Tell them to meet us out by the carriage."

"Very well," the servant said and left.

Malagant turned to the king.

"Lancelot is here."

"Then we are ready," the king said, and then he and Malagant left to rejoin the receiving party.

Victoria was straightening the folds of Guinevere's dress, and Maerwynn was in front of the mirror, finishing brushing her hair. In the mirror, she saw the glimmer of her necklace and rolled it between her fingers to watch it sparkle and flicker.

"Guin, why is this so last minute, this visit? How come we had no notice?" she said.

"I just found out this morning, too."

"So, what's going on, then?" Maerwynn persisted.

"I don't know."

"I believe something good might come out of today," Victoria said as she continued to smooth out Guin's dress.

"What do you mean?" Guinevere said and brought her hand down to halt Victoria's primping, but Victoria just looked up at the queen and gave a dry smile.

Chapter 14

Lancelot and Perceval had been intercepted by Malagant's servant and changed course to proceed out to the stables. They didn't say a word to each other. Their professionalism had taken over, and they were now playing at being knights.

Guinevere, Maerwynn, and Victoria were also headed out to the stables, and they also walked in silence, turning the various corners in unison, their dresses brushing the hard stony ground. But upon coming to the final passageway to where the carriage was waiting, Guinevere had just turned her head and saw out of the corner of her eye Lancelot approaching from an intersecting direction. While Guin kept walking, half puzzled by seeing the knight, Lancelot immediately stopped, and then Perceval, too, halted.

"What is it?" Perceval said, looking around.

"The queen walked by," Lancelot said, in full honesty.

Perceval relaxed.

"Of course. She's going on the picnic, as well," and he let his eyes linger to catch Lancelot's response.

Guinevere and the girls emerged into the sun and passed through the enumerable lines of guards and accompanying nobles to where the royal carriage was waiting. Maerwynn and Victoria parted from Guin and went to one of the other carriages, but Guin saw the king's carriage and as she was rounding the cabin to her doorway, she looked up and saw Sir Sebastian sitting atop next to the driver. Her eyes lingered on him for a moment, for she had never seen a man with such dark polished skin. His hair was like the thick coat of a wild animal, and he was perched with such a confident posture, reclining on the wooden seatback, that Guin thought of him as an exotic animal sunning himself on a mountain outcropping. But she continued on to the door, and looked back for a moment to the line of coaches and saw her sister and Victoria getting inside the one behind hers.

Before opening the door, she looked through the window. Arthur was already inside, sitting across from a strange looking woman. When Arthur saw his wife, he reached over and pushed the door open.

"Where's the man escorting you out?" he said and looked outside for the absent servant. "No matter. Here, come inside." Guin entered and sat next to her husband. "Queen Guinevere, may I present Princess Adelina. Princess, my queen, Guinevere."

"Very nice to meet you," Guin said and they exchanged a delicate handshake.

Guin couldn't help but study the Princess. Her hair was as black as the man's sitting on top of the coach, and her skin equally as polished. And how ablaze her eyes were, so shimmering brown that they seemed like a lost treasure glistening beneath a surging ocean surf. When Guin saw the Princess' clothes, like a metallic cloth, draped over her shoulders, she looked down at her own dress and thought how unfortunately simpler her fabric was. And the woman's long boots, what were they made of?

"Your boots, very nice," Guin said, trying to make conversation.

"Is that alligator?" Arthur said

"Not quite," Adelina said, absentmindedly looking out the window. "It's imitation alligator. Made out of one hundred percent crocodile."

The line was delivered with such casualness that Guin began to further study the princess. She was beautiful, sure, but in a different way from the queen, a way that Guin was only now realizing was possible. While Guin was sunshine and lightness and fairness, all the ways that beauty was defined in England, Adelina was shadows and mystery and sat there opposite her with a kind of stern, confident charisma new to Camelot, at least new for a woman. Lancelot, with probing glances at the various carriages, appeared at the door, but before saying a word, turned to see Perceval and Gawain getting into a coach, the very one Maerwynn and Victoria boarded, although he, of course, had no way of knowing that.

"I heard there was an open seat in this one," he said, still standing outside but looking in through the window.

"Yes," Arthur said and pushed open the door. Lancelot momentarily glimpsed up at the strange knight sitting atop the coach, and then got in and sat next to Adelina, across from Arthur and diagonal from Guinevere. "We were just remarking about her boots," Arthur continued. "What do you make of them?"

The knight saw the waxy brown skin and the green scales.

"What is that, bunny rabbit?" Guin openly laughed, and Adelina looked over at Lancelot and then down at her boots, stretching them out for better viewing. "I was talking about the lining on the inside," Lancelot corrected.

"Oh, you can see through crocodile skin?" Adelina said.

"Yes, I can see through skin."

"Sir Lancelot, this is Princess Adelina. Princess, Sir Lancelot, my finest knight."

As Arthur introduced them, he put his hand outside the window and banged on the door. Instantly the carriage jolted forward and they were off.

"Princess, you'll forgive me," Lancelot began, "but you are princess of what kingdom?"

"Valencia."

"Where is that?" Guin asked.

But as Arthur started to answer, Lancelot, in the

natural momentum of the conversation, said, "It's well beneath France, to the west, on the Mediterranean. Ah, Princess, that is quite a long trip, and I did not even know you were coming," he said, and looked up to make eye contact with Guin.

She, sensing Lancelot's point—why she hadn't told him last night—spoke: "Yes, I, too, only found out this morning." And she returned Lancelot's look.

"I was in the area, and when Arthur found out, he extended an invitation, and I obliged."

"And I was told you, a princess, are a trade emissary?" Lancelot asked, looking at her hands and seeing her rings. "Those are nice rings for a trade emissary."

Adelina's fingers were lined with rings, from large jagged amethysts to oval emeralds—the full spectrum of colors. When Guin heard this, she curled her hands into the fabric of her dress to hide them. With her single wedding ring, she could hardly compete.

"She is a princess, after all," Arthur said, "and I think the rings are very befitting."

"Thank you," Adelina said.

"Well," Lancelot said, "let me see," and reached out to her hand. "If I may," and Adelina obliged and let him make her hand into a fist. "Now imagine throwing a punch with these finger knives coming at you." He brought her hand around as if in a swing. "See? Let us make no mistake about why women wear rings."

Adelina laughed, and Guin did, too. Arthur sat there uncomfortably.

With her hand still extended, Adelina asked, "And which gem is your favorite?"

Lancelot looked over her collection of rings.

"I don't see it here." He sat back. "I've always been partial to bloodstone." He looked over at Guin. "Bloodstone. Your Highness has heard of it? It has little red specks in it, little red dots."

"Little red dots, I have seen it," Guin said.

"Yes, and that is my favorite."

This little allusion to the night before, when the tree thorn had sprinkled her dress with blood, began in Guin a new series of thoughts about Lancelot, for what kind of man would, in the midst of speaking with a beauty such as Adelina, return his mind to her? And his comment with the secret meaning was not just a casual allusion. It was made in the presence of the king, and that made all the difference.

"Her boots, though," Arthur said to Lancelot, "clearly they are one of two animals, the alligator or the crocodile. But which one would say they were?"

Lancelot took but a moment to glace down to come up with an answer.

"The crocodile, of course."

"Please tell me," Adelina said, sitting up. "How did you know?"

"Yes," Arthur repeated, "how did you know?"

"Simple. Comparatively, an alligator has a broad snout, but her foot is slender, like the snout of a crocodile. Princess, you will forgive me for using the word snout."

They all laughed, that is, except Arthur, who sat there quiet and self-conscious. Maerwynn, too, sat quietly in her carriage. Next to her was Sir Gawain, and across from her, jostling with the rumbling motion of the coach, were Victoria and Perceval. Out of the corner of her eye, Maerwynn was spying the shiny bracelets around Gawain's wrists. She was fascinated with the intricacies of one in particular, as it was in the shape of intertwining copper ropes. Victoria saw Maerwynn's downcast glances and grinned. She nudged Perceval, who saw the same thing and thought it was cute and innocent.

Lancelot also jostled with each bump of the road. The talk had momentarily died down, and Lancelot's eyes moved from the countryside outside the window to Arthur, who seemed to be checking the weather, to Guinevere, who, to his surprise, was looking directly at him. Lancelot shook his head as if to suggest that she should look elsewhere. Guin shrugged. Lancelot nodded.

"So, Princess Adelina," Lancelot began.

But the princess interrupted him.

"You can call me Adel."

Guinevere shot her a look, but Adel had her head turned.

"Adel. I was wondering. That is a very fancy dress you are wearing, very ornate, undoubtedly very expensive. Let me ask you. We are going to a picnic. Going to eat a lot of different foods, could get very messy. If something drips on your dress, some sauce or mustard or something, would you try to wash it out or would you throw the dress away? Because as princess, I'm sure you have a lot of dresses and could easily replace it."

"No, No, "Guinevere said. "Don't influence her. Let her answer it."

"I was only saying," Lancelot said.

"Because I'm sure, as a princess, as you put it," Guinevere said, "she probably has the very best cleaning supplies, some cleaning solutions, maybe some washing contraptions and such."

Adelina watched as the queen and the knight went back and forth. Was she noticing something? Arthur sat motionless.

"Well," the princess began, "I might try to clean it, and if it came out, good, and if not then I would throw it away."

"So you would try to clean it, first?" Guin said.

"But then you'd throw it away, without remorse," Lancelot added.

"And as you were cleaning it," Guin said quickly, "you would really hope the stain would come out, and try sincerely to clean it and not just rub some water on it."

"Actually," Adelina said, "dirty or clean, I'm probably only going to wear this dress once, like I wear all my clothes only once, and then discard it and wear something brand new tomorrow."

Lancelot and Guinevere were having trouble making her answer fit their sides.

"So...you are saying you will throw it away," Lancelot said as if the final answer had been given and he was the winner of the argument. "Good, then it's settled."

"Nothing is settled," Guin quickly said. "The question is still open."

Arthur leaned in.

"What question had to be settled? What are you two talking about?"

Arthur was clueless. He didn't get it. Adelina saw the awkwardness and spoke up.

"Sir Lancelot, or is it Lance?"

"Lancelot. With all due respect, Lance is a little familiar." And he looked at Guin and gave a sly smile. Adelina saw this.

"Lancelot. I was thinking of taking up using the sword...."

"Do you mean using the sword or fencing? Because one is about killing and the other is mere art."

"Killing?"

"Again, with all due respect, Princess," he said and drew his sword. "Look at this blade." She reached for his sword, and he pulled it away. "Please. I sharpen it to slice through flesh. Do you know how many men this sword has cut in half?" Lancelot's tone was light rather than serious. "How many arms I've lopped off that have fallen and gotten buried in the mud? How many throats I've slashed and watched the heads swing back?" Lancelot sheathed his sword. "I don't know what we're having for lunch, but perhaps I can interest you in one of the knives that will used on the strawberry preserves?"

"Point taken," Adelina said and touched him on the arm. Guin saw this and then looked out the window.

Back in Maerwynn's carriage, Gawain was struggling to pull his sword out of his scabbard. It was stuck. Perceval and Victoria could barely contain their laughter.

"No," Gawain said, pulling at the hilt, "Maerwynn, you really must see this. I have embedded rubies in the sword blade itself. I don't know why it won't release. Eight beautiful rubies. Ah."

The procession of carriages rolled along the road, beside the green pastures, with rocky hills in the background. The sun was reaching its high point in the sky. Trees now and again cast shadows in the cabin, and as Guin followed a shadow moving across her arms, she saw again how white her hands were and how smooth. Then Guin looked up and saw Lancelot watching her, and she quickly checked Arthur, who was, again, gazing out the window. Returning to Lancelot, she turned her palms up, and Lancelot raised his eyebrows to acknowledge that, yes, they were white and clean. Adelina spoke up.

"Now that the wars are over, Arthur, what is the one issue you now have to concern yourself with? If I may ask, because we have the same problem in our kingdom."

Arthur wondered how she could pinpoint the very crisis he was now confronted with. And for her to bring it up, he also wondered how he could agitate her and provoke a war when she herself seemed to know his very predicament.

"Well," he said. "I suppose, to put it bluntly, peasant uprising and revolution."

"Yes, that is our issue as well," Adelina said. "But, as one of our court mathematicians said, the king should never fear a revolution."

"Not fear a revolution?" Arthur didn't understand.

"A revolution, as our mathematician said, is a complete, circular rotation. Think about it. A revolution, by definition, is movement, certainly, but when all is said and done it ends up in the exact same point. So, the king is in power, there's some commotion, and then, in the end, the king is still in power. That's a revolution, by definition. Otherwise, if we end up in a different point, what would that be? I don't know. A corkscrew or something." Arthur didn't know what to make her theory. "That makes sense, doesn't it, Lancelot?" Adelina asked.

Lancelot was still studying Guinevere's hands, but he then looked up.

"Have you convinced the peasants of this, that what they really want is a corkscrew?"

Adelina laughed.

"Hah, the dreaded peasant corkscrew...and we know how they like to whine," she said and laughed at her own joke.

Lancelot politely smiled, as did Guinevere. Arthur continued to look out the window.

"And what kind of hands do you have to have to turn that corkscrew?" Lancelot added and looked at Guinevere.

Soon there was a rap on the ceiling of the carriage and the procession stopped.

"Ah, we are here," Arthur said without enthusiasm. "But we still have a slight walk ahead of us. Our spot is just over the hill," he said, pointing.

Sir Sebastian, who had been riding atop the carriage, opened the door for the four passengers. When they got out, Adelina said to Arthur," May you walk with me if your queen permits it? Guinevere, you wouldn't mind if Arthur escorted me and you walked with Lancelot?" Guin, a little surprised, slowly nodded. "Good," Adelina said and slipped her hand under Arthur's arm. Guin turned to Lancelot, who stood there as if this were the expected natural run of things.

The servants unloaded the baskets of food and the blankets, the cutlery, the plates and dishes, all the supplies for the picnic. It was a big production, as numerous knights and nobles were in attendance. As the horses were being tied up, Lancelot turned to Guin, "Did you want them to give you a lesson on how to tie up a horse." Maerwynn and Victoria, along with Perceval and Gawain, got out of their carriage and proceeded to follow the rest of the pack, which included Sir Kay walking arm-in-arm with two maidens, other knights, Malagant, and even Sir Lionel who walked alone.

Lancelot and Guinevere walked on up ahead, following a faint path which had appeared and skirted the sharply descending slope of the mountainside.

"So," Guin said, "Princess Adelina is certainly pretty, isn't she?"

"I suppose so," Lancelot said, matter of factly.

"It's fine, you can say it."

"Sure, she's pretty."

"I thought you would think so."

"Sure, but there's more to a woman's appeal than being pretty."

"And her personality, she's witty," Guin added.

"She is witty, yes. But there's more to attraction than beauty and personality."

Guin was skeptical.

"Is this where you play at being deep?" she said.

"Play?" Lancelot gave an appreciative nod. "Can I show you something?" And when Guin seemed to go along with his gesture, "Look," he said, pointing toward the valley below. "Now, sometimes it is there, sometimes it is not. It is up to you. Tell me what you see?"

"What I see out there in the distance?"

"Yes. Describe it."

"Well, I see the mountain peaks, the grassy slopes,

the little river running around the bend. Maybe those are animals grazing on the hillside, I'm not sure."

"Keep going."

"Uh, the grassy pasture gives way to a thicker meadow, the clouds hover over the peaks, the sun streaks the valley in light and shadow."

"Is it beautiful?"

"Yes, it is."

"I agree. It's absolutely beautiful. Now," Lancelot continued, "put everything together. Not its parts, but what else is there with it as a whole?"

As Guinevere squinted into the valley, Lancelot made sure they were making good progress along the path, ahead of the others. She thought, trying to access her feelings, but it didn't help. Her eyes narrowed, scanning the distant mountain slopes, the gaps in between the peaks, the whole of the scene. And then she slowly realized what else was there.

"I think I see it. I mean, I don't know, but something else is there. It's like, um, um. It's like.... I don't know how to say it." She looked at Lancelot. "I can't put it into words."

"Right. And that's how I know that you and I are seeing the same thing. That, whatever it is, is the thing beyond beauty and personality, absent for me in Adelina, the thing that convinces us, well, that we are in love."

"In love? We?"

"The other day, when you, me, and Maerwynn were about to talk about love, this is why I objected. If you put love into words, then it's not really love. It's mountain tops and pastures, not that other thing that we can't describe."

"But Maerwynn talks about it all the time. Love is like a floating cloud and stuff like that."

"Like? She uses a simile or metaphor and approaches love from an angle, indirectly. See, she can't take it straight on."

Guin turned and again gazed into the valley. Arthur and Adelina were still many paces back, and they looked on at the knight and the queen.

"What do you suppose they are talking about?" Adelina said.

"I know my wife well," Arthur said. "Look at her. She's probably guessing at distances, at how far the opposing mountains are from here, how wide the valley is. Look at the view. How can anyone be talking about anything else?"

Maerwynn and Sir Gawain were walking together.

"Courtly love is one of the most stable and reliable enterprises today," Gawain said, speaking as if he were a teacher. "And so the skill set involved is one that everyone can practice and perfect. The key is to know what to do and when to do it. Upon coming of age, every young woman should be issued a handkerchief. And we should all put in extensive time learning the business of composing poems of love, for expressing our feelings, making them concrete and clear, that is how we know we are in love." Gawain started to shake his head, agreeing with his pronouncements. "Yes, yes, love poetry is perhaps the finest of pastimes, for it is what separates us from the beasts. But how about you, fair Maerwynn, what do you do? Do you write poetry perchance?"

Sir Kay still had two maidens on either side.

"Sixteen or seventeen," he said. "I was with two other knights and we all unloaded our arrows into the canyon. But which of us got the death blow, I cannot be certain. So modesty keeps me from saying seventeen. But definitely sixteen dragons."

Perceval and Victoria walked off to the side.

"Sure, I've been coached in courtly love, in how to address women." Perceval said.

"Women, plural? No," Victoria corrected," one should learn not how to pick up women, but a woman, singular. We are all different."

"Oh, I know."

"Of course you do." Victoria was soft and sweet and motherly, and Perceval felt good to walk next to her. He felt calm. "So," she continued, "how do you know how to relate to a single woman?"

"You talk to her...like we are talking."

"Yes," and when she agreed, the knight smiled.

Lancelot and Guinevere kept their lead ahead of the pack.

"But," Lancelot said, "how did you know to come to Ryerson Hall?"

"Victoria suggested it. She said she knew you'd be there."

"But I never go. I only went because Perceval dragged me there."

"So Perceval made you go?" the queen said.

"And Victoria made you go?" Lancelot answered back.

They looked at each other, and it clicked in them simultaneously. At once, they both looked back at their two friends and saw they were walking shoulder to shoulder. Perceval and Victoria immediately saw the gaze.

"Why do you think they're looking at us like that?" Perceval said.

"Because they know what good people we are," she said.

Arthur continued his conversation with Adelina.

"Most likely two day's journey across, maybe three, and then 4 day's wide, I am sure of it. I know my kingdom well."

"I certainly see that you do," Adelina said patronizingly, put her arm under his once more as they walked, and looked up to Lancelot and Guinevere.

The picnic was set up on a bluff overlooking the valley. Servants spread out blankets for sitting. Baskets full of bread and meats and butter and jams and smoked fish and olives and fruits, all the food befitting a royal picnic, were placed in the middle of each blanket. The king and Guinevere, who had rejoined him and Adelina, sat around on the one of the larger plush blankets. Guin, sitting now, pushed down on the blanket to feel how soft the grass was beneath the blanket. Lancelot, joining them, said, "Everyone is like that underneath." Guin smiled. Sir Sebastian settled on a neighboring blanket with some nobles. Maerwynn and Victoria sat with Gawain and Perceval nearby, and the knights and nobles covered the rest of the crest of the hill overlooking the purpling valley. Maerwynn was looking at all the pretty glass jars and bottles, thinking which one she would add to her collection. She reached for an ochre-colored mustard pot.

Lunch was served, partially by the servants and partially by the people helping themselves to the baskets. Lancelot didn't eat. Instead he lay on his back and curled the edge of the blanket over to shield his eyes from the sun.

"Lancelot," Adelina said, with a glass of wine in her hand, "surely you will join us for lunch?"

The knight peeked out from under the folded blanket, and seeing the glass of wine in her hand, "Was that opened by the peasant's corkscrew?" And without waiting for a response, he returned to his sleeping position.

More food was served, including pastries, of which Adelina took multiple helpings, placing them on the blanket around her. Maerwynn continued to talk to Gawain, and while Guin couldn't quite make out what they were saying, judging by Gawain's elaborate gestures, she could tell their interaction wasn't exactly casual. Guin caught Maerwynn's eye, and Maerwynn motioned to meet her away from the group. Guin excused herself and joined her sister behind a clump of bushes.

"Guin, I just met the most fantastic knight."

"Sir Gawain?"

"Yes. He is incredible. Smart. Has all kinds of interesting ideas. And look at him, how he looks. I've never seen a knight dress like that. And the stories he tells. In my mind I've already written, perhaps, ten poems about him."

Maerwynn was beaming, and Guin could only say, "Wow."

"I think...I think...I'm in love. I know I only just met him, but he's just so incredible. He's handsome and the way he talks to me. And he likes poets, and when I told him I was a poet, we talked all about poetry. Love, I think it's love. Guin, do you think it could be love?"

Guin remembered what Lancelot had said about love, that reasons could not be given for it. But this was her sister.

"Just take it slow."

"Do you believe in fate? Guin, do you think it's fate."

"I don't know."

"A sign. Maybe if there was another sign."

"Maybe." Guin didn't quite know what to say, but knew they shouldn't be gone too long. "We should get back."

And as they were returning to the group and about to go to their separate blankets, Maerwynn said, "A sign is what I need."

"Sure, yes," was all Guin could say.

When Guin sat back down, Adelina scooted over next to her.

"So, Guinevere," Adelina began, "Arthur was telling me on the walk here that Maerwynn is you sister. Was that her?"

"Yes."

"And what does she do?"

"She's a poet."

A look came over Adelina's face.

"I'm sure your sister is very nice, but a poet? We had a poet back home, also a girl, and...well.... A poet's job is to feel, because that's what they do, write about how they feel. And poets, in accessing their feelings, often times manufacture those feelings, create them, in order to live up to the gravity of their poetry."

"I can see that."

"But tell me," Adelina said with a smile. "Maybe princesses and queens are like that, too. We feel the need to live up to our station."

"Our station feels the need to live up to us," Guin added, and then looked over to Arthur, thinking that perhaps she shouldn't have said that. But Arthur wasn't paying attention, lost as he was in the perspectives of the widening valley. Lancelot sat up.

"The way that knights aspire to become men," he said.

"And the way poets aspire to become human. Guinevere, ask your sister where her reality is, on the outside or on the inside." Adelina looked closely at Guin. "Or you. As a queen, you have everything, and all that's left is to want more of what you already have. Poets want their outer world to look like their inner world, and queens, I'm sure, want their inner world to look like their outer world."

Guin thought about that for a moment, and then said, "Sure, Maerwynn is different than me."

"No," Adelina quickly said. "Maerwynn is different from me. From not than." Guin gave her a blank stare. "It's directional. Think of it that way. Different from me. You from me," she said, making hand movements to and away from her body. "When I say that King Arthur is different than Sir Lancelot, the direction is moving not from me but out there, between them. So I would say King Arthur is different than Sir Lancelot, not from Sir Lancelot. You see the difference?"

"Oh," Arthur perked up. "How are we different?"

"What do you mean?" Adelina said.

"For the sake of the example, how am I different from Lancelot?"

There was a moment of silence. Malagant, eating an apple, was approaching, and having heard the question, leaned against an adjacent tree. This was a dangerous question, for it was for Adelina, a discerning woman, to articulate the differences between her husband and Lancelot in front of Guinevere. She, now, the visitor, could say what Guin would never dare voice. And if Guin wasn't already thinking what Adelina was about to say, she would certainly soon be. Arthur had other thoughts, not about what his wife may hear, but about what the people around him would hear Adelina say about himself, the king, for of course all ears where on the conversation of the king. And, for Arthur, this might provide the very disparaging words that he could use as a reason to go to war. Lancelot motioned to Perceval to come over, and with him Victoria, Maerwynn, and Gawain. Arthur looked quickly at Malagant, nodded, and Malagant took the clue.

"Yes, Princess Adelina," Malagant said, "for our amusement, what are the differences you see between Sir Lancelot and Arthur, King of Camelot?"

Perceval and Victoria exchanged puzzled glances. Lancelot and Guinevere looked at each other, as Arthur seemed suddenly alone with his own expectations.

"The differences between the two," Princess Adelina began. "First was the comment, when we first met, about what my boots were made of. While Lancelot guessed they were made of bunny rabbit," and as she said that there was laughter. Arthur looked around to see where it was coming from, and she continued, "Arthur thought it was alligator."

Adelina paused. "Now while it seems that Lancelot's comment was funnier, wittier, showed more of a quickness of mind, I prefer Arthur's seemingly throwaway line. Why? Because he allowed me to make my joke: When he said alligator, I said no, they're imitation alligator, one hundred percent crocodile. You see, Lancelot stole the spotlight, and Arthur, in his magnanimity, let me be the star and say the funny line. So, here, I prefer Arthur."

Arthur didn't quite know what to make of her comment. She had said Lancelot was funnier and wittier, and people laughed, but had ended up preferring him, Arthur. It was an insult, and people saw that, but she had covered herself at the end. He had no room to object. How could he turn that into a provocation for war? Arthur looked at Adelina, then to Lancelot, and then to Malagant, who only shrugged. Adelina continued.

"And my rings. You all see them," and she fanned her hands out so all could examine her rings. "Lancelot thought they were to serve as small knives when I might strike someone." People giggled. "But Arthur said they were very befitting a princess." Again, you see Lancelot stole the attention for himself with his astute observation. But Arthur returned the praise to me. And that is their difference and why I prefer Arthur, his generosity."

Once more, the compliment was made to the king, but the public's approval was with Lancelot. Arthur sat there, dumbfounded, and Guinevere, for all her mixed feelings, didn't know quite what to make of Adelina's comments. Certainly, they focused her attention on the disparity between her husband and Lancelot. But, if anything, they were sentiments she had already been entertaining, if not in such an articulated form. And was Arthur generous in the way in which Adelina was describing? Guin wasn't sure, but she did know they were different. It's not that

Adelina was correct in her assessment, but that a very real assessment could in fact be made, and that perhaps Guin herself should start to add up all the ways in which Lancelot was different from the king, a notion that she had already noticed but not fixed in her mind. And did Lancelot already say they were in love?

Malagant was still leaning against the tree, still eating his apple. He had held his tongue long enough. With a flip of the wrist, he tumbled his half-eaten apple into the grass. He walked over to Arthur and whispered into his ear.

"Your Majesty, may I have a word?" and he and Arthur separated themselves from the others. "I really must say something."

"I know already."

"You know?"

"That you think there is something going on between Guinevere and Lancelot."

"Yes."

Malagant was shocked, for how could the king have anticipated his objection. But he had to subdue his reaction in mixed company.

"And, Sire, you allow it?"

"There is nothing to allow. There has been no real proof."

"But surely if you suspect something...."

"And there will be no war with Princess Adelina."

"And now no war?" Malagant couldn't understand.

"I cannot send men to their death."

"You can and you have."

Arthur looked around to make sure no one had caught on to their conversation.

"But not over this. Enough. Enough."

"But the villagers, the people? And Lancelot?"

Arthur thought for a moment.

"What we need is more proof," and with that he detached himself from Malagant and returned to the group. "To honor Princess Adelina," he announced to everyone, "we will now have a display of skill and courage. From four of our knights, we will have a contest of swordsmanship. Two pairs will battle, and the winners will then square off." Arthur scanned the knights lying on the blankets.

"We will have, first, Sir Perceval spar with Sir Kay, and then Sir Gawain spar with Sir Lancelot, and then the winners." When Lancelot's name was announced, Guin sat up and turned to look at Lancelot. Malagant saw this and whispered in the king's ear. Then Arthur declared, "And the winner will receive a kiss from our fair Queen Guinevere." Guin was stunned, but looking at Victoria and then at Maerwynn, she quickly hid her alarm. "Let's clear out a circle here," the king said, signaling to move some of the center blankets aside. And he directed to a servant, "Please retrieve four wraps for their swords."

"What's your plan, Sire?" Malagant whispered.

Arthur pulled Malagant aside.

"With the prize being a kiss from Guinevere, if, seeing how hard Lancelot fights, he wins, that will be our proof."

"I do not understand."

"Lancelot will fight to win in order to kiss her. Then we'll know."

Malagant paused.

"But Sire, won't Lancelot win no matter what. After all, he is the best knight." Arthur breathed heavily and looked up at the passing clouds, now knowing his plan was ridiculous. "And," Malagant continued, "all you've done is allow Lancelot to kiss the queen, and to kiss her with your consent, and in front of everyone."

Arthur hung his head. No war with Adelina and now the Lancelot-Guinevere kiss, nothing was working out. But he had to go along with the tournament. It was already under way. The four knights slowly got up, a little surprised, but their professionalism surfaced, and they adopted, for show, an attitude befitting their knighthood. Lancelot, Perceval, and Gawain quickly put their heads together.

"We know we have nothing to prove," Gawain said.

"So you should win," Lancelot said. "Gawain, I saw you with Maerwynn. For her, you should win."

"Yes, I agree," Perceval said.

"But Kay will never go along with it," Gawain whispered.

"I'll take him out legitimately," Perceval answered, and when he saw Kay approach, he said, "So we'll put on a good show."

"Yes," Kay said, "a good show."

The servant returned with wraps for their swords, and the knights took them and started to cover up their blades so that no metal was showing, thus protecting anyone from getting seriously hurt. As Perceval and Kay got into position, taking a couple practice swings and stretching, Lancelot and Gawain went to sit down on a blanket neighboring Guinevere's. Lancelot made eye contact with Guin and then turned to Gawain. He whispered a few words while looking around at the food containers spread out on the ground around him. Arthur, still standing near the sparing circle, was next to Malagant.

"Malagant, you announce the knights. You run it. I cannot."

As Malagant began to introduce Perceval and Kay, Arthur returned to sit next to his queen and Adelina.

"This ought to be interesting," Adelina said in all earnestness. She really was looking forward to it.

Lancelot leaned in close to Gawain so no one would hear him say, "What are we, the entertainment? I thought we were warriors."

"Times change," Gawain responded

"Here, we have Sir Kay," Malagant said to the crowd, and some cheered. And here, Sir Perceval." More cheering, a little louder. "Let me check the wraps so that no sharp blade is exposed." He touched each man's sword to make sure the wrap was secure. "And now, the first man to conquer the other wins. Men, on your mark. When I drop my hand, you will tap each other on the chest with your swords to show the blades have been dulled, and then begin." Stepping away, Malagant dropped his hand and the two knights exchanged light blows to the chest. Perceval looked over at Victoria and playfully shrugged. Then, as Sir Kay held his sword in front of him, Perceval wound up and swung his sword crosswise and snapped Kay's sword clean in half. Kay froze. The audience was silent. Perceval unwrapped the cloth from his sword and put the sword back in its scabbard. Then he walked back over and sat down next to Victoria. Malagant returned to center ring.

"I guess we have a winner. Sir Perceval," he exclaimed. The audience clapped, now recognizing Perceval's feat. Kay slumped back to his blanket. Malagant announced the next contenders.

"Princess Adelina," Lancelot said, passing her on the way to the circle, "did you see that? Before a knight who knows how to wield a sword, there is no defense." He continued on, tightening the wrap around his sword.

"Here, on this side is Sir Gawain. And on this side, Sir Lancelot. When I drop my hand," Malagant said, giving the directions, "tap each other on the chest with your swords, and then begin." Again, after checking the wraps, he dropped his hand. Lancelot touched his sword to Gawain's breastplate and then whispered, "Hard." Gawain, hearing this, put a little extra on his sword tap, connecting in the center of Lancelot's chest. But as Gawain crouched to begin the fight, Lancelot fell to one knee, let go of his sword, and clutched at his heart. The audience gasped. Gawain looked on in dismay. Removing his hand from his chest, Lancelot revealed a palm full of what looked like blood. A hush came over the people. Lancelot rose to his feet and, half stumbling, staggered over to the king's blanket and fell to the ground before Princess Adelina. Seeing the look of terror on Guin's face, Lancelot, short of breath, reached for Guin and wiped red on her hand, saying, "The red spots got me." And with that, he rolled over on his back. Arthur rushed to Lancelot's side. Guin looked closely at her hand and saw strange lumps in the red. She smelled it. She then tasted it. It was raspberry preserves. She smiled a smile of relief. Surround by concerned onlookers, Lancelot, out of the corner of his eye, saw Guin's expression change. Without a care for those rushing to his aid, he sprung to his feet and stepped into a small clearing in between blankets and bowed.

"I hope you all were entertained," he said and the crowd cheered. And then with sarcasm, "Because we are the entertainment. Thank you," and he bowed to the crowd, "Thank you."

Upon returning to the blanket, Adelina said, "Well done."

Arthur, after his initial alarm, sat in silence and gave a blank stare to Malagant. Perceval joined Gawain in the sparing circle.

"Now let's put on show," Perceval said.

While Malagant was introducing the two knights, and once Lancelot had noticed that the concern for him had died down, he said to Guin, "Sorry." Guin gave him a look to show she was slightly upset for having been teased and for thinking that something had happen to him. "But how is your hand, still white and clean?" She showed him.

"Raspberry preserves wipe off plenty easily."

Lancelot leaned forward to catch Adelina's attention.

"Princess," he called out. "I can give you your first knife lesson if you like?"

Adelina smiled back. Perceval and Gawain had started their fight, and the crowd watched as the knights swung the swords round and round, over each other's heads, making lunging stabs, listening to the muted clangs of their wrapped blades.

"Two crosses and under sweep," Perceval whispered. And they crossed swords right-on-left and then left-on-right, and the Perceval made a low slashing motion, over which Gawain leapt high in the air. They whispered their upcoming moves, and so could dazzle the crowd with daring swordplay without there ever being any danger. And so lunge after lunge went on, all with deadly quickness, and the onlookers oohed and awed with each sword clash.

Adelina leaned forward.

"Yes, Lancelot, perhaps jam knives are more my style."

The fight went on until, exhausted, Perceval allowed a light glancing blow to impact his shoulder, thus making Gawain the winner. But the fight had been a success. The crowd had been entertained, and both knights shook hands and bowed to the people. Lancelot, looking up at the bright afternoon sun, had an idea. He called out to Malagant to wait to announce Gawain winner. Quickly, he got up and ran around to all the knights that were circling the area, giving them directions. After he made his way around, he sat back down and began to unwrap the cloth from around his sword. Once done, he gave Malagant the go-ahead to declare Gawain the winner. And as Malagant held Gawain's hand in the air, Lancelot and all the other knights drew their swords. They angled the blades to catch the sunlight and directed the glare to Gawain. Suddenly, from the light, Gawain's armor burst into a chromatic display. The shiny metal on his shoulders refracted the shimmering light in all directions. The rubies in the blade of his sword glowed fiery red, the emeralds in his belt glowed, and the diamond studs in his breastplate shot the sunlight out in all the colors of the rainbow. Lancelot nudged Guin to look over to her sister. Maerwynn was spellbound as Gawain was radiating with all the colors of the spectrum. She couldn't move. Arthur had had enough. He got up and made a circle with his finger in the air to Malagant, letting him know it was time to go. With that, Arthur went over to Victoria and pulled her aside.

"Do you know what just happened, with Lancelot harnessing the sun like that? He linked the Heavens and the Earth," he said and walked away without waiting for a response.

The sun was starting to set over the distant mountains, and the shadows off the mountains stretched toward the procession—the servants carrying the picnic supplies, Maerwynn with her newly beloved Gawain, Victoria with Perceval, and the new partnering of the King with his Queen, and Lancelot and Princess Adelina. With Lancelot, back at the picnic when he was lying on the ground, there were moments when he began to question what he was doing there. And his actions, half flippant and not fully thought out, demonstrated this. How he faked his stabbing and was unable to think of a good way of playing it off to Guinevere after her initial shock, how virtually inanimate he was lying on his back with his hand over his eyes when colorful words would have amplified the situation in his favor. Presently, walking next to Adelina, he felt how heavy his chainmail and vest had become, how heavy his shield and sword.

"I'm thinking of moving back to France," he disinterestedly said to Adelina.

"Why would you ever do that?" she responded. "Here is where you belong."

"I came here to simplify my life, and now...."

"Here is where you belong," she said again, widening her eyes as if to communicate something.

Lancelot shook his head.

"Princess, what you're talking about is why I left France in the first place."

Adelina reached out and touched his arm.

"And, Lancelot, what am I talking about?"

They both smiled, for Adelina's perceptiveness was almost a welcome relief for Lancelot. There was no need for him to explain anything.

"Then you see why I must leave."

"Do you always run from a challenge?"

"Leaving is a testament to my loyalty to Arthur."

"And what about your loyalty to yourself?"

"I'm a knight. My loyalty has been pledged elsewhere."

"You give up your freedom in order to avoid it."

"I'm a knight."

"To give it up means you once possessed it."

Lancelot looked her in the eyes.

"I'm a knight."

"Don't you want to be happy?"

"I will sleep well tonight."

"Because you are going to run away," Adelina said, letting out a long exhale.

"I'm going to leave as a way of executing my allegiance to the king," Lancelot said, blankly looking straight ahead.

"What about your allegiance to the queen?" Adelina said.

Arthur walked with Guinevere. Lost in thought, he was silent, trying to put together new ideas. The king looked back and saw Malagant, then saw Victoria walking with Perceval. He turned to Guinevere.

"I think we're going to need some more research," he said. Guin nodded. "Tonight, when we get back." Then he turned to Malagant, who caught his eye, and nodded to him.

Chapter 15

Later that night, Malagant met with Arthur.

"You wanted to see me," Malagant asked.

They were alone in the king's chamber.

"Yes. I have a new plan."

"A new one?"

"Thought of it when we were walking back to the carriages."

Malagant looked around.

"What is your plan?"

Arthur took a deep breath.

"Guinevere is going out tonight. And she will be kidnapped."

"Kidnapped? Guinevere?"

"The Wazee tribe, I've contacted them to kidnap Guinevere and take her to the old abandoned Larimer Castle. But no one is going to hurt her."

"What do you mean?"

"This is all a plan."

"But Your Highness, what are we suppose to accomplish by this?"

"After she is taken, I will send you, Lancelot, and Perceval to rescue her. The Wazees will allow you to rescue her. Then you and Perceval will separate from Lancelot and the Queen, allowing them to be together. That will allow them to develop the kind of closeness we are trying to prove." Arthur saw Malagant's expression of disbelief. "Don't you see? This will create the proof that we're after."

"Arthur," Malagant whispered, as if to a child, "why are you trying to build the very relationship you are trying to prevent?"

Arthur took a step back and looked up into the

recesses of the room.

"You cannot destroy something that doesn't exist. We have to make sure it exists first."

"But why can't you just stop it from beginning?" Arthur was getting flustered.

"Sir Malagant," he said calmly, "I am the King, and you will do as I say. You, Lancelot, and Perceval will go rescue her. Nothing bad will happen. And then you and Perceval separate from them. That's what I want."

Malagant was quiet.

"Yes, Your Highness."

Malagant marched off, and King Arthur, alone now in his chamber, sat down quietly in a chair and hung his head. But then he got up and walked off.

"A dark sash, wear it like this," Maerwynn said.

"And this to hide your face," Victoria added, draping a black shawl around her neck and shoulders. "Back to Ryerson Hall?"

"Yes."

"So I should tell Perceval to tell Lancelot again?" Victoria said.

"Please do," Guin said. "And Victoria, maybe I should have known, but you and Perceval?"

"I know," Maerwynn said.

"There's something strong and yet vulnerable about him. He's confident in some ways and defenseless in others."

"Sure, compassion and sympathy need a weakness to latch onto," Maerwynn said and Guin looked at her, impressed with her eloquence.

Victoria and Maerwynn continued to adjust Guinevere's wardrobe when they heard a knock at the door. Victoria answered it. King Arthur stood there with a small satchel.

"May I speak with the Queen?" he said.

Victoria, with her eyes set on the king's hesitant

expression, stepped aside. As the king entered, he waited quietly until Maerwynn and Victoria got the hint that they should leave.

"I just wanted to make sure everything was ready for tonight," he quietly said. Guinevere went on with preparations. "And here," he said, taking from the satchel a small folded cloth. Unwrapping it, a portion of chicken and cheese were inside, as was a second small cloth covering a large handful of cherries. "In case you get hungry."

"I can wait until breakfast tomorrow."

"Just take it. In case." Guin rewrapped the food and put it inside a fold of her dress. "And do you think you might need something heavier? It might get cold out."

"It's fine out."

"But it might get cold."

Arthur grabbed a coat from a nearby rack.

"Just wear it. For me. You never know."

He draped it around her shoulders. Guin pulled it tight.

"You're being awful nice to me," she said.

"I can't be nice to my wife?"

Guin paused.

"You're right. You can be nice."

She gave him a sly look.

"Nice is the wrong word. Who wants to be described as nice?"

Guin continued to get ready, adjusting her head scarf, securing the wrapped food.

"How about when I get back, I'll have a new word for you?" she said.

Arthur knew this was a mistake. Guinevere was heading towards the door.

"Just hurry back," he said.

She gave him a quick kiss on the cheek and smiled.

"I know nice isn't the right word."

Arthur was silent as she left.

Camelot, too, was quiet that evening. As Guin road to Ryerson Hall, it was hard for her to hide the smile on her face. Perhaps Lancelot would be there, though she did not know that Victoria had been unable to find Perceval. And so Lancelot, having reconciled to leave for France in the morning, was preparing his bed beneath the oak tree. He gathered in the loose grass and had put on an extra layer of clothing to protect him from the cold. Guin secured her horse and entered the hall. Her disguise was perfect. No one would recognize her. A bench was open on the side wall, and as she sat down, she scanned the crowd for a familiar face. Lancelot's shield was beneath his head as a pillow. He stared up through the branches at the clusters of stars. Seeing only strangers, Guin eyed the doorway. Lancelot crossed his feet and put his hands behind his head. Guin waited and waited. She passed on drinking and ignored those looking to talk. The crowd noise, for her, became overwhelming. Finally, convinced Lancelot wasn't going to show, Guinevere gathered her things and left. Outside a carriage was waiting and, absentmindedly, she passed before its opening. A hand reached out and shoved a cloth in her mouth, pulled a hood over her head, and then lifted her in. No noise was made. The front of Ryerson Hall was as quiet as Lancelot's meadow, for he was now fast asleep. And the carriage slipped away into the night.

King Arthur strolled down the corridor, lost in his torturous thoughts. The moon shone in through the windows, and in and out of the light he went. Victoria, who had been looking for Perceval, turned into Arthur's path.

"Oh, excuse me, Your Highness," she said.

"No, no. It is I who should be excused," Arthur said, and as he walked slowly away, Victoria stood there watching. Her natural impulse was to follow him and try to help and find out what he meant, but she knew whatever it was, the king's concerns were his alone. So, she remained in the hall, motionless, following Arthur with her eyes. But then Arthur stopped. In the stillness of the castle, another set of eyes was on her—the now confused eyes of Maerwynn. She couldn't hear Victoria and Arthur's words, but what she had recognized was something more certain, their sharing of sympathies. And the poet in her knew that was a more powerful exchange, even a dangerous one. Maerwynn saw all she needed and now turned and hurried to bed.

Queen Guinevere, beneath the blackness of the hood, could only hear the rumbling of the carriage wheels. She didn't struggle, not to free herself, not to spit out the gag in her mouth. Instead, she was calm, and let the events take their course while she gathered her thoughts.

Maerwynn, in bed, lay still. A candle perched in a wall sconce flickered and sent little shimmers of light across her array of colored bottles. She listened for footsteps in the hall, which she would know would be Guinevere's returning from her nightly excursion. But she heard nothing.

Guinevere was taken out of the carriage and marched in through the big double doors of Larimer Castle. With her hood still on, the blackness made more prominent the creaks in the wooden doors she passed though, the smoothness of the stone stairs she climbed, and the murmurs from her captors. They were careful not to say anything concrete so as to give any clues. And so when Guin, after a long climb up what seemed to her narrow stairs, was finally shoved into a chamber and had her hood removed, she was left not knowing where she was or who had kidnapped her. With her vision restored, she made her way to the window, which was barred. But because of the thickness of the wall and angle of the window sill, she couldn't see the ground below her, only, high as she was, the tops of the trees and the black horizon beyond the forest. She slouched down in the corner, on some hay that lay strewn about. Her cell was small, and when she pressed her hand to the stone walls, they were cold and rough. No light was visible from under her cell door. She got up and went to listen for noise coming from out in the hallway. But all was silent. She was surprised at her composure, that she wasn't panicking. Why, she thought, was she so calm? Was it because she knew Arthur would come rescue her, or because Lancelot would? It was useless to ponder such questions, in part because she sensed she was immediately taking sides. Who would she prefer burst through her cell door? She felt a bulge in her side, and then pulled out her bundle of food. In the darkness, the cherries were black. She put a piece of bread in her mouth and curled up in the hay.

Lancelot had slept in, and even the livestock grazing in the adjacent field hadn't woken him. Perceval rode up on his horse.

"Lancelot, wake up. Arthur wants us."

Lancelot gathered his shield and untied his horse from a nearby branch.

"You know I'm going back to France today."

"Did you tell the king that?"

Lancelot mounted his horse.

"I would never presume to tell him anything. I will ask his permission to leave. I'm still in his service until he releases me."

"Well, he wants to see us. You can ask him then."

And with that, they galloped off to the castle.

Maerwynn lied in her bed, awake, taking in, as she usually does, the colored spectrum cast by sparkling bottles. There was a knock at her door.

"Come in," Maerwynn called out.

The door opened slowly. It was Victoria. She just stood there.

"Victoria, come in. You don't look so well. Are you alright?"

Victoria approached and sat on the bed.

"There's something I have to tell you."

"What is it?"

"Last night, something happened."

"Oh?"

"I don't quite know how to tell you."

"Victoria, just say it."

"It's not good."

Maerwynn sat up.

"I know what you're going to say."

"You do?"

"Yes, I saw what happened."

"You did?"

Victoria was shocked.

"It was dark, and I couldn't really hear anything. But I saw enough."

"Then you should tell the king," Victoria said.

"Tell him?"

"Yes. If you saw your sister get kidnapped, why didn't you say anything?"

Maerwynn froze.

"Kidnapped? Guin got kidnapped?"

Now Victoria froze.

"Last night, yes. She never came home."

"How do you know she never came home? Kidnapped?"

"Yes. Then what did you see?"

Maerwynn was silent.

"We need to see the king."

In a small chamber, Arthur sat with Malagant, waiting.

"Are you sure this is a good idea?"

Arthur looked at him and sighed.

"There are no more good ideas."

"Then why are we doing this?"

"Because we have to do something. And here, take

this." Arthur handed Malagant a small satchel of gold coins. "You'll give this to the leader of the Wazee tribe. He'll be expecting it."

"I have to deliver it?" Malagant said, but then Perceval entered with Lancelot, and Arthur launched into the proper attitude while Malagant hid the satchel.

"Lancelot, Perceval, I have a quest for you two, with Malagant, and word of this cannot get out."

But just then, Maerwynn and Victoria burst through the door.

"Where's my sister?" Maerwynn said. The alarm in her voice struck Lancelot.

"What's going on?" he said.

"Now stay calm. Everything is going to be fine," Arthur said. "Maerwynn, your sister has been kidnapped."

"Kidnapped?"

"We're going to get her back. Lancelot, Perceval, and Malagant are going to go rescue her."

"We are?" Lancelot said. "If the queen is missing, why aren't you sending the whole kingdom after her?"

"Because that would provoke a war. And we just got done with one."

"If this isn't cause for a war, then I don't know what is."

Malagant interrupted.

"I think we should just do what the king says."

Lancelot gave him a stern look.

"Listen, Lancelot," Arthur said calmly. "Either we can worry the whole kingdom, and take the time to gather in all the knights and the whole war machine, or we can not waste any more time and make the effort now."

"Do they want a ransom?" Perceval asked.

"No. No ransom," Arthur said.

Lancelot looked over at Maerwynn, who couldn't speak. She was still in shock. All this talking, this needless discussion, wasn't getting them anywhere.

"Where is she?" Lancelot said.

"Larimer Castle. The Wazee tribe is holding her," Arthur said.

"Then we should leave right away."

"But listen. This is not to get out. No one is to know."

"Your Highness," Maerwynn said, "what about Sir Gawain? He could go, too."

"No. Just these three."

"But certainly…."

"Just these three. Now, we're wasting time."

"Yes, we should go," Lancelot said.

"I know where Larimer Castle is," Perceval said.

The others nodded and then, without another word, went down to the stables to gather their horses. Maerwynn started after them. This gave Arthur the space to lean into Victoria.

"I need to talk to you. Excuse Maerwynn," the king said.

Victoria went over to Maerwynn, who was standing in the doorway.

"Victoria," Maerwynn suddenly said, before Victoria could speak, "I must take care of something." And without waiting for a response, she ran off. Victoria turned to Arthur and shrugged. The two of them, alone now, went over to the window. Down below, they could see the knights readying their horses.

"Victoria, I must ask you something in confidence," Arthur said.

"Of course."

Arthur thought for a moment and then said, "Are Guin and Lancelot having an affair yet?"

Victoria didn't quite know what to say.

"Yet? You expect that they will?"

"What I mean," he tried to correct, "is, are they…how should I put this? Is it official that they are together?"

Victoria looked into Arthur's eyes. She could see he was struggling with his emotions.

"Yes," she quietly said.

"Good," he said.

"Good? This is good? This is what you want?"

Victoria didn't understand. Arthur winced and covered his face with his hands and gritted his teeth.

"No, not good. And not what I want. But I have no choice."

"What do you mean?"

"Victoria...Victoria...Victoria." Arthur took a deep breath. "We don't live in an ideal world. There is no such thing. All we can do is make the best of a broken world."

"What's broken? I don't understand."

"You're the only one I can talk to. You have to understand."

"But Sire, what is broken?"

He didn't know how to explain it, and the concrete reasons he couldn't share. So he looked around the room, scanned what he was wearing. Then, coming to an idea, he pulled out a small knife from his cloak. Victoria didn't move.

"Take this. Take this knife." He thrust the handle of the knife into her hand. When she gripped it, he held it there. He was breathing heavily and was becoming somewhat frantic. Arthur then pulled up his shirt, exposing the flesh of his stomach.

"Now, I know I'm going to be stabbed. But I have a choice: to be stabbed once or twenty times. And the sooner I'm cut, the sooner I can heal. Do you get it?"

"Who's going to stab you? You have no enemies?"

"Oh, Victoria. Time will stab me."

Maerwynn was rushing in and out of the rooms in the castle. She ran out to the courtyard. She borrowed a horse and galloped through town. And in Ryerson

Hall she found Gawain.

"Gawain, Gawain," she said. The knight put down his drink and was escorted by Maerwynn outside.

"Gawain, Guinevere has been kidnapped, and you have to help get her back."

Gawain, like Lancelot, assumed his proper role as knight.

"Where is she?"

"Larimer Castle. Lancelot, Perceval, and Malagant are already on their way."

"I'll join them."

"No, you cannot. Arthur only wants the three of them going."

"Then what would you have me do?"

"Follow them. Remain unseen. Rescue my sister."

"I will leave at once."

Maerwynn was surprised at his willingness and at how he didn't question anything.

"You will do this?" she said. "Even though the king has not chosen you?"

"Of course. I'm a knight and my allegiance is decided. No one will tell me I cannot rescue my queen, not even the king."

"But if the others see you, they will know I betrayed Arthur."

Gawain thought this a simple point.

"Then I will stay unseen."

As Gawain started off, after a few paces, he turned around and went back and stood in front of Maerwynn. "And what about my allegiance to you?" He leaned in and kissed her. Maerwynn demurred. "And maybe a poem would be in order for the occasion." And with that, he rushed off to his horse, mounted it, and galloped away.

As Maerwynn stood there in front of Ryerson Hall, she called after him, "Be the hero!"

Guinevere sat in her locked chamber. Without any

candlelight and only the sun for illumination, the confines of her imprisonment seemed not entirely unpleasant. There was ample straw to set down over the cold stone floor. She didn't see any rats about. An early morning breakfast was provided. Still, she was being held captive. It went through her mind that her kidnappers were only after a ransom, and so it would be a mere formality of just waiting it out. And so she sat there, peacefully. But sitting soon led to boredom. No noises were coming from outside in the hallway. She couldn't see very much outside her window, as high up as she was. But maybe she could do something. So Guinevere walked around her room, pressing up against the stone walls with her hands, inspecting, looking for weak points. The ceiling was high and there was nothing around she could stand on to get a closer look at the upper corners. But, from what she could see, there wasn't anything out of the ordinary in their construction. It seemed like a normal chamber, sealed off to become a prison. She flopped back down on her straw. In doing so, she felt again the lump in her clothes and pulled out the little package of food. Guin picked through it, and when she came to the cherries, she held them out in her hand. They were red, and she made a connection. Red dots, like she and Lancelot had shared. Maybe she could do something with them. She poured all the cherries out into her palms and walked over to the window and dumped them out. They all fell down to the ground below, directly under her window. Then she lay back down on the straw, resigned to wait.

Lancelot, Malagant, and Perceval were on their way to Larimer Castle. Each was on horseback, not galloping but in a quick trot. Perceval and Lancelot exchanged looks, and then Perceval spoke.

"And you were going to leave to go back to France?"

Malagant heard this.

"You were?"

"We can't stay here forever," Lancelot said matter-of-factly.

"But you were going to leave us and return to France?" Malagant asked, trying to figure what this could have meant to Arthur.

"If Arthur would have released me from my service, yes."

"You would have asked his permission?" Malagant continued.

"Of course. I am in his service."

"And if he had granted you your wish, you would have left?"

Lancelot looked at him as if these questions were none of his business. He was calm but stern, and whatever he was thinking about Guinevere, there was no indication on the surface.

"I'm doing my sworn duty to the king and queen, and that is all."

Perceval heard this and internalized these words.

"Just your duty?" Malagant asked, recognizing an opening to see if he could find out anything more.

"Three knights against a whole tribe, only duty would compel me to walk into such numbers."

Malagant puzzled over this, as did Perceval.

"What do you mean numbers?" Perceval asked.

But Malagant saw a different angle, that of objective duty.

"Is it duty alone that compels you?" he said.

"Wait. What numbers?" Perceval didn't like the sound of that.

Lancelot looked at one and then the other.

"The Wazee Tribe, they're known as the Knight Killers. I thought they were in France, but apparently they've now crossed the Channel. I can name twenty French knights they've killed."

"But those were French knights," Perceval said. "I can handle myself. And you, Lancelot, no one is getting the better of you." Then he and Lancelot looked at Malagant. "Sir Malagant, I've never seen you handle a sword."

Malagant didn't know what to say.

"You question my ability? You, Perceval, think I'm not fit to be a knight?"

"I said no such thing. Only that I've not seen you in battle."

"And Lancelot, you, who were all set to run away? You, who...." Malagant held his tongue.

"Me, who what?" Lancelot said. "Who what?"

Malagant didn't want to be so blunt.

"You, who knows only duty, who is only following his loyalty to his king and queen."

"Yes, that's right. Loyalty to the king and queen. My pledge is my bond. Perceval, you told me this once. 'If it needs must be.' And that is why I'm here. Guinevere has been kidnapped. She must be freed. That's it. If it needs must be."

"You're confident against numbers?" Perceval said.

"I am."

Malagant turned away and gave a look of horror.

Guinevere sat in her chamber. Her prison ceased to amuse her and she was lost in her thoughts. What could she be thinking about? Just then, a slot in the bottom of the door opened and a tray of food was slid in. It was lunch. She looked at it and then glanced out the window. Maerwynn lay in her bed, alone, resting on her elbow. In her hand was a quill. She was composing her poem for Sir Gawain. Out loud, she tried various combinations of words.

"Ease and trees. Pleasantries. A forest of pleasantries."

Gawain, knowing the route to Larimer Castle, soon caught up with the three knights. Not wanting to be detected, he hung back, and rode behind them. He felt awkward spying on them. But, duty bound both to Maerwynn and to the help ensure the safety of the queen, he knew Lancelot would understand.

King Arthur was with Victoria. They were alone. Before them, spread out on platters, were various cuts of meat and bread and vegetables, an array of fruits and berries, bottles of wine. They had just finished eating.
"Victoria, can I tell you something?"
She sat up and moved closer to him.
"Of course."
"I mean, can I tell you something and you tell no one else?
"Not even Guinevere?"
"Certainly not."
"What is it?"
Arthur took a deep breath.
"Who is missing here?"
Victoria thought for a moment.
"What do you mean?"
"To whom would I normally turn in a crisis like this?"
She thought again and shook her head.
"Merlin," Arthur answered.
"But where is he?"
"Gone. He left as soon as Guinevere and I married. What I'm about to tell you, no one knows." He gathered his breath. "He said that if I married her, she would have an affair with Lancelot and cause the downfall of Camelot."
Victoria gasped.
"Merlin predicted it?"
"No, not a prediction. Fate. Marrying Guinevere sealed my destiny and that of Camelot to one of failure and ruin. And Merlin couldn't bear to watch that happen, so he left."
"But why don't you just keep them apart."

Arthur's voice became intense.

"Action? No, it is fate, and nothing I do can interrupt that."

"So what can you do?"

Arthur sat back.

"Hurry fate. Make fate arrive rather than avoid it. When Lancelot didn't attend my wedding, I had to make sure they were later introduced. I know Guin has been going out at night to meet Lancelot. I know everything. But enough was enough, and whatever obstacles may be in the way, loyalty, duty, allegiance, I had to force the connection. That's why....I orchestrated Guinevere's kidnapping so Lancelot could play the hero and accelerate their romance."

"You did what?"

"Victoria, don't you see? Necessity will play out, and the faster it arrives, the faster it can be put behind us. Camelot may fall, but what new kingdom will rise in its place? And to what greatness will I ascend to after this trial is over? When one effort is ruined, another may begin. Don't you see?"

"But why did you marry Guinevere in the first place? Why didn't you just take Merlin's warning and call off the wedding?"

"We can control our actions, but not our emotions. And why didn't I just control my actions? I did. I could no longer take wrestling with my heart, and my choice of action was to acquiesce to a heart bent on ruining me. I may rule a kingdom, but I cannot rule my own heart. The fight now, toward an impending fate, is winnable in that I may control the tempo of its losing."

"You must hate Lancelot."

"Because I am powerless against him. And not in terms of the greatness of his being, but only as it is decided by the narrow gaze of Guinevere. I envy no one, have want of nothing. But the faintest pregnant sigh by my queen gives birth to an unimaginable hell."

"Then what must you do?"

"Ready the conditions for rebuilding." He breathed heavily into the air. We must hurry the affair in order to expose it. Love has never saved anyone."

"Love hasn't?"

"Love has only built the battleground on which we all will meet our demise. Love sharpens the swords of others. Love readies our flesh for the impaling. And when we fall, love removes the rocky ground beneath us and we descend into the unending abyss."

"But you talked about the ascendency into the next kingdom?"

"That's the outside world. What we can see and touch, what we can cling to, what we can pull ourselves up with. The invisible, love, that is what pulls us back down. No king has ever been defeated in the visible world."

"Kings lose wars all the time."

"They may lose the war, but the defeat is long before, elsewhere, inside."

Maerwynn scribbled some new lines on the parchment, and said them out loud: "And the old silver-tongued mists that enter the room and make the forest for us. That wanders and needs and looks and leaves, that we use for the bricks of our temples and our love."

Gawain made his way through the early afternoon mist that suspended itself among the branches and dampened the ground. Gawain wiped the moisture from his sleeves. He could see the three knights traveling in the partial clearing between a bank of trees and a row of tangled thicket. They were speaking, but he was unable to hear what they were saying.

"Perceval, you call nature a she, but why?" Lancelot asked.

"Mother Nature. Mother is a she."

"OK. Tell me about Mother Nature," Lancelot continued.

"You need only look around," Malagant interrupted. "This mist, what is it for?"

"What is the mist for?" Lancelot repeated.

"Yes," Malagant said.

"It is not for anything."

"Certainly it is," Malagant corrected. "It is to blur our way, to impede us. This mist is here for us to fight through."

"So that we," Perceval continued, "may strengthen our resolve."

Malagant took over: "May revisit and renew our certainty about completing this quest."

"Right," Perceval said. "All goals have obstacles."

"And the obstacles, as we fight through them, serve to intensify our focus on the goal. You see, Mother Nature is helping us by impeding or progress."

Lancelot balked.

"And if the air were clear, you'd say Mother Nature was testing our, what did you call it, resolve by making quitting so tempting and easy."

"No," Malagant said.

"Sure. You'd say that every gap in the trees is a potential exit. You'd say that Mother Nature put a row of open doors in front of us to strengthen our certainty and intensify our courage to open the locked door behind which Guinevere sits."

Guinevere paced back and forth. If something was going to happen, then let it happen, she thought. Enough of this waiting. She looked out her window and could see only the bunched treetops. She rubbed her arms to warm up. The afternoon chill had arrived. She took a deep breath.

"And you hear all the time," Lancelot continued, "about how nature blesses us with a good harvest or smites us with a storm that batters our houses. But nature isn't benevolent or mean. It doesn't help or hinder us on purpose. We call it an angry wind or a gentle breeze, but they are not. Why do we do that, endow nature with human attributes it does not otherwise have?"

"To better understand it?" Perceval said.

"To be able to relate to it?" Malagant said.

"No. We grant nature human traits in order to believe it might possess the whole spectrum of emotions. Why? Because that allows nature the capacity for love, so that it might love us. For that gives us a solution for one of the most harrowing of human tragedies, to love while unloved."

Perceval and Malagant were quiet. They were turning over that thought in their minds. And then Malagant spoke.

"And so, what, you would rather have us act against nature, as Gawain does, piling jewels upon jewels, affection upon affectation? To love nature? He is against nature."

"Well, we all are," Lancelot said.

"But Gawain, shiny this and shiny that. He has gone so far that if not for diamonds and shiny metal, the sparkles, we wouldn't even recognize him."

"Watch your tongue," Lancelot interrupted. "There is no one more loyal, more dependable, than Gawain."

Gawain, unseen atop a nearby ridge, continued to follow at a safe distance. Maerwynn lied among her parchments and colors and poetic thought. Arthur and Victoria reclined among their tray of fruit. And Guinevere, cold, covered herself in straw and drifted off to sleep.

With Gawain trailing and out of sight, the three knights descended a shallow ridge valley, and that's when they saw Larimer Castle through the trees. They surveyed the scene. They didn't see a patrol out. In fact, they saw hardly any sign of the castle being inhabited. It had no drawbridge, no moat. They couldn't see any smoke coming from inside, as if no fires were going for warmth. But perhaps the thin layer of fog would have obscured the smoke. From their cover, all they could see was a few guardsmen overlooking the top of an exterior wall.

"She could be anywhere," Malagant said. "I say we split up. Perceval and I will go around to the left. Lancelot, you follow the wall around to the right."

Without a word, just a look, they all nodded, dismounted and tied up their horses. Malagant and Perceval, staying within the cover of trees, hurried away into the fog. Lancelot put his hands out as if to test the moisture in the air. Gawain, seeing them part, decided to stay with Lancelot. And the fog gave him cover to stay close. Off his horse now, Gawain, as a precaution, walked along with his sword drawn. Lancelot, however, securing his sword and the quiver of bow and arrows on his back, kept his hands out as he emerged from the tree cover and approached the castle wall. With visibility down to a few yards, he felt following the perimeter of the wall would be the best way to find a way in.

Malagant and Perceval soon saw what looked like a door embedded in the castle wall. Malagant patted himself to make sure the pouch of gold was still there. It was.

"Stay here," Malagant said. "I'll go check it out."

"I'll go with you."

"No, you stay here and see if anyone comes up behind me."

"We're a team."

"I'll signal for you."

Perceval shrugged.

As Malagant neared the door, Perceval wondered

why his sword wasn't drawn. "Draw you sword, draw your sword," he kept saying. But when Malagant was at the door, he simply pushed it, and it opened. Without looking back, he entered. No signal.

"Eh, what are you doing?" Perceval said to himself, drew his sword, held it in two hands, and ran after him and through the door.

Gawain tried to stay as close as he could. He could see Lancelot walking with his back to the wall, checking for a way in while looking forward and back for oncoming Wazee guards. And that's when Gawain saw a Wazee ahead of him watching Lancelot. He was a few paces ahead of Gawain, and the curving tree line gave him a good view. Gawain, seeing that Lancelot wasn't aware he was being tracked, quietly snuck up behind the guard and slit his throat. His action was so clean and without build-up, one was reminded why Gawain was a knight in the first place. Not because of how shiny he was or the jewels in his sword, but because of loyalty and prowess. With the dead Wazee lying on the ground, Gawain saw a chance for a plan. He quickly stripped out of his knight's armament and put on the plain brown clothes of the slain, including his lambskin hat. Now, Gawain would be able to pass as a Wazee and maneuver through the castle to find Guinevere. He relocated Lancelot, who was still edging the perimeter wall.

Lancelot was careful not to step on any branches or twigs that would snap and make noise, and so he was constantly looking down. And that's when he saw something on the ground, a bunch of them: the cherries. "Cherries?" he said to himself. "Why would cherries be here?" And then he thought: "Red dots." He stepped back and looked up. There was no opening in the wall, but up above there was also no walkway, only an isolated tower, a tower with a high distant window. That's were Guinevere was, and he knew it. Lancelot stood there a moment, looking out into the forest. Gawain stood still. There was something in Lancelot that welled up, but he was unsure if it was the passion of loyalty or something else. But if there was even a question, then he knew it wasn't just loyalty. Why couldn't everything go as planned? Why couldn't he be on his way back to France? He reached down and took one of the cherries and fastened it to the tip of an arrow. Then he took his bow, pointed it up to the distant window barely visible through the fog, and fired the cherry-tipped arrow into the window. Then he placed his hands on the stone wall and began to climb.

The arrow shot in through the window and clanged onto the hard stone floor. Guinevere awoke. She looked around and saw the arrow. She picked it up and plucked the cherry from the point. She smiled. She knew.

Gawain, once Lancelot was sufficiently high enough, went a ways down and began to scale the wall himself. He saw where the arrow went, and he knew what it meant. But while Lancelot proceeded with confidence, finding secure foothold and grips, Gawain repeatedly slipped on the fog-moistened stone. At least with his knight's uniform off and instead wearing the clothes of the Wazee, the climbing was made easier.

On the other side of the castle, Malagant went down corridor after corridor. Perceval followed. He wanted to call out to Malagant, but he couldn't risk it. So he hugged the walls and stayed in the shadows.

Lancelot, knowing that no rescue was possible through the narrow window, climbed over to where the walkway was, and rolled over the top lip into a darkened corner. He was in. Guinevere was in the tower on his left, so he went in that direction until he came upon a door. Gawain, too, reached the walkway. He was breathing hard. Dressed as a Wazee, he could blend in with any patrol that went by, so he hurried around to the right. In a door, down some stairs, and then quickly, he passed Lancelot on the level below. He passed a Wazee, nodded, and kept going. His disguise was working.

Malagant made his way into a gathering chamber, encountering a group of Wazee, who drew their swords. Perceval nearly walked out into the group, but caught himself and hung back. But he could hear them.

"Easy, easy." Malagant slowly reached inside his cloak and pulled out the pouch of gold. "I have the payment from King Arthur to secure Queen Guinevere's release."

"Ah," said one of them. "Stay here. I will go get someone."

As he ran off, Malagant sat down in a chair.

"There were no incidents finding her, were there?" he said.

"No, no. Outside the hall, she was there. No one saw us."

"Us, you say. How many are there of you are here? It's my understanding you came over from France."

"A small number. Forty or so."

"There are forty of you here in this castle?" Malagant asked, now standing.

"Securing it so more may make the trip."

"Forty? I think we can handle forty."

"Handle?" the Wazee said.

"Yes." And with that Malagant drew his sword and sliced his interlocutor through the stomach, then spun around and chopped the head off another. By that time, the third Wazee had drawn his sword, but Malagant, with ease, knocked his weapon to the side and ran his blade through the man's feeble brown leather vest.

Perceval winced at this. It took all his strength to resist emerging from his hiding spot and cutting down Malagant with his sword. But he couldn't stay where he was. So he took a deep breath and ran out. Malagant spun around.

"Malagant," Perceval said, "I heard the commotion from down the hall. What happened?"

"Good, you're here. One ran off to get reinforcements. They're going to come from there," Malagant said, indicating a doorway on the far said of the room. "We'll get on either side."

They both stood, swords at the ready, beside the doorway, waiting. Perceval glared at Malagant, tightening his grip on his sword.

Gawain climbed a set of stairs, and knowing that a tower as narrow as this could only have a single room at the top, when he came to the single door he knew it was her chamber. Through the peephole in the door, he looked in. Indeed, Guinevere was right there, still with the arrow in her hand. Gawain looked back down the stairway to make sure no one was coming. It was clear, so he took out his sword to pry open the lock. What Gawain didn't see, though, was that Lancelot had made his way up the stairs behind him, hidden by the way the stairs wound around the circular tower's inner perimeter. Sword out, held in two hands, Lancelot crept. As he came around, he saw, from the back and without seeing the man's face, the drab brown Wazee clothing. Sword out, he sliced the back of the man's knees, and as Lancelot was about swing and sever his head form his body, he saw the sword with rubies in it. And as the man dropped and spun around, Gawain's face came into plane view.

"Oh Gawain, not you," Lancelot said under his breath.

But Gawain passed out, and Lancelot, in his haste, stepped over his fellow knight and kicked the door open. Guinevere was standing there, cherry and arrow in her hand.

"I knew you'd come," she said, giving a slow smile.

Lancelot's face was without expression. He simply

grabbed her hand and ran with her down the stairs, though he did not see Gawain, who, he figured, must have been dragged off by a Wazee.

Slicing through men, piercing, tearing, kicking aside the severed limbs, Malagant and Perceval carved through the Wazee Tribe. Perceval, with the strength of his full swing, cut men in half as they poured through the narrow doorway. Malagant, with his lunges, punctured lungs and kidneys, hearts, spilling the intestines of the kidnappers. The Wazee were no match for the knights.

"We have to get all of them. No one must survive," Malagant said.

Perceval gave him a strange look as he continued to slash away. With all the noise, every Wazee was drawn to the chamber and thus to their deaths. The knights, covered in blood, turned the scene into a farce, for it became an exercise. Moving from room to room, the Wazee were killed, one after another. There were no challenges, no competition. As the blood-spattered, not one blow struck them. And when all the Wazee were dead, they turned around and walked out.

"What about Guinevere?" Perceval said.

"I'm sure Lancelot found her." Exiting the castle, Malagant and Perceval saw Lancelot and Guinevere hurrying along the tree line. "See," Malagant said, and then he and Perceval ran to join them where they had tied up their horses.

"We must split up in case they come after us," Malagant said.

"But I think we killed them all," Perceval said. "There is no one left to come after us."

"You killed them all?" Guin said, surprised.

"All of them," Perceval repeated. The knight looked at Guinevere and then at Lancelot. He knew he had to tell what he had heard, that Malagant was in on the kidnapping, but could not bring himself to tell the whole truth. "Malagant was supposed to pay them off, but he kept the money, and we killed them all."

"There was a payoff?"

"The satchel of gold is under his cloak."

"Does Lancelot know?"

"I don't think so."

"Good. Please don't tell him. I will handle this."

And with that, the queen and Perceval returned to the two other knights, who were standing beside their horses.

"We should go," Malagant said. "Your Highness, you ride with Lancelot, and Perceval and I will get any who come after us."

"Malagant," Guin said in an appreciative voice, "I want to thank you for helping to rescue me." And she went over and gave him a hug, just so she could feel and confirm the existence of a gold satchel beneath his cloak. For cover, she also gave Perceval a hug and whispered in his ear, "Thank you."

"Princess," Malagant said, "you and Lancelot should get going. We will see you back at the castle."

Guinevere and Lancelot mounted his horse and rode off. Riding, Guin wrapped her arms around Lancelot and put her head on the back of his shoulder. How could the king have orchestrated her kidnapping? What did it mean? And Lancelot, over and over in his mind, he thought about Gawain. What was his involvement? And how could he ever admit to killing Gawain, and did he kill him? He could not be sure?

Through the forest they galloped, across the grasslands, into another thicket of woods. Soon, to give his horse a rest, he dismounted, leaving Guinevere as the sole rider, and took the reins and walked beside his horse.

"Guinevere, may I tell you something?"

"Of course. What is it?"

Lancelot thought for a moment.

"What I would like to tell you is that I know something that I cannot tell you as of yet. And I'm asking you not to press my loyalty and make me disclose it. When something comes out, this will be that, and I want to tell you that I would never keep anything from you...."

"Without telling me what you are talking about?"

"Right."

"I understand. But what if I were to tell you that I already know."

"You do?"

"I might."

"If that is the case," Lancelot went on, "then I would ask that we keep it from each other so that we each might maintain the possibility that the other doesn't know and is thereby not affected by it."

"Lancelot, you would like to pretend that we don't know what we know?"

"Not quite. I would like to act as if I am wrong, even thought I know I am right, and the only way I can do that is if you do not confirm the truth of what I know. And, of course, if I don't confirm the truth of what you know. Does that make sense?"

"It does. But may I ask you about what you believe?"

"You are the queen."

"Very well. Do you believe in fate?"

"Whose fate? Fate in what?"

"In general."

Lancelot kicked at the forest leaves. Everything was silent.

"For me, fate does not exist, because it doesn't matter if it exists. If I am fated to do this or that, and I do not know what this or that is, then what does it matter?"

"But do you believe things are meant to happen?"

"Purposefully?"

"Yes."

"Well, yes. But only in way, after the fact."

"What does that mean?" Guinevere asked.

"Have you ever heard a minstrel's song take a particular turn in the melody and think that that is the only place the song could have gone?"

"Yes."

"But you only think that after your hear the musical progression. Or, your sister writes poetry. Do you ever, after you hear her rhyme two words, think that, of course, that second rhyming word was coming?"

"Sometimes her words seem a little contrived."

"So, yes, I believe in fate, but only insofar as after something happens can you work backwards to construct a lineage to prove how certain, how fated, that that particular something was to happen."

"I understand, but that's not true. Once I threw the cherries out the window, that's when I knew you would rescue me. Beforehand."

"But how did you know I would come for you? Truth be told, I had very different plans for today."

"No. I knew. I'm Guinevere and you're Lancelot. Who else can rescue me but you?"

"My duty. Now, we will not talk until we return."

"No talking. That is ridiculous," she said, but Lancelot did not respond.

Guinevere rode atop the horse, with Lancelot walking in front, holding the reins. Neither said a word.

Malagant and Perceval, now recovering from their exhaustion, lumbered on their horses. They were a short traverse of a ridgeline away from descending into Camelot.

"We should wash this blood off," Malagant said. "The last thing we want to do is give the initial impression that something went wrong and set off an alarm regarding Guinevere."

"That something bad happened? Do the

townspeople know?"

"I don't think so, so we wouldn't want to raise any suspicion that king doesn't have his house in order."

"Then we should wash this blood off, you are right."

Both knights dismounted and knelt down by a nearby stream. They proceeded to rinse off their swords and douse their armaments. Their shields were cleaned, their hands scrubbed, and breastplates polished.

"What happened back there, anyways?" Perceval said. "Did they rush you, or...?"

"When I came upon the first guy, there was some commotion, and then he sounded the alarm. That's how I knew they were going to be running in through that doorway."

"Good thinking, because we must have caught them unaware. It's like they weren't even prepared for us."

"Well, that's why we're knights and they aren't. Now, do you still doubt my skills with the sword?"

"No, I do not doubt."

"And maybe when we get back, we shouldn't tell Arthur that we killed the entire Wazee tribe. I mean, how would that look? It wouldn't be befitting a knight to have death seem gratuitous, would it?"

"No."

"So we should just say 'quest accomplished.'"

"Quest accomplished?"

"And spare Arthur the gory details. What he cares about is his queen. So, quest accomplished?"

"Quest accomplished, indeed."

Perceval didn't like it.

Arthur spoke casually to Victoria on his balcony.

"But what kind of world will it be?" Victoria said.

"I don't know. A quiet one, I hope, one where our castle will sit quietly on a hilltop overlooking a wide sweeping valley and where the land will be wide open and the fields will abound in crops and livestock."

"That sounds nice."

"Doesn't it? Where snow covers the mountaintops and the melt water runs into brooks teeming with fish. With fields of clover and lilac and where we awake to minstrel songs celebrating my beneficence."

"Yes, that is the kind of kingdom in which I want to live."

"Then that is the kind of kingdom we will have. And indeed, I already have a place in mind."

Before another word could be said, he heard the faint knock on the inside door.

"Your Majesty," came a voice through the door.

"Uh. Victoria, stay here."

Arthur went in and answered the door. It was a servant.

"Your Majesty, the queen and Lancelot have arrived. Should I show them in?"

"Um." Arthur couldn't think fast enough, and before he could answer Guinevere and Lancelot burst in through the door. Victoria remained hidden on the balcony.

"Arthur!" Guinevere said and threw her arms around him. Lancelot looked the other way. "I'm sorry, I'm sorry. They surprised me and...."

"It's fine. It's fine. The important thing is that you are back now, unharmed. They didn't mistreat you, did they?"

"Mistreat her?" Lancelot said under his breath. "They kidnapped her."

"No, nothing happened. They just locked me in the tower."

"Until Lancelot could save you," Arthur completed. "Ah, my best knight."

"It was my duty," Lancelot said dryly.

"Surely it was more than a duty?" Arthur said.

"I am a knight and she is the queen."

"And I am the king, and I say tonight we shall have a grand ball with music and dancing."

"Oh, that would be just lovely," Guinevere said.

"Just lovely," Lancelot quietly echoed, and then in stomped Malagant and Perceval, all clean and shiny and proud.

"My lord, quest accomplished," Perceval exclaimed.

"Quest accomplished?" Arthur said, looking at Malagant.

"Yes, Your Highness," Malagant quickly said.

"Quest accomplished," Perceval repeated. "Lancelot, quest accomplished. My queen, quest accomplished. My king, yes, quest accomplished." Perceval threw up his hands, and turned and slowly walked away, saying, "Did we accomplish the quest? Yes. Quest accomplished."

"I will talk with him," Lancelot said, and as he went after Perceval, the king called after him.

"There will be a ball tonight. Dancing!"

"Yes, Your Highness," Malagant picked up. "It all went according to plan, and," glancing over at Guinevere, "the queen is back in your safe keeping, I am glad to say."

"Very good, Malagant. Now, if you will leave me to my queen."

"Yes." And Malagant turned and left.

"Now, Guinevere," he started to say, but then Guin began to walk over to the bed.

"I am so tired. I need a moment to lie down."

Arthur panicked.

"Perhaps visiting your sister to reassure her of your safety is in order," Arthur said in a hurry.

"Yes, maybe you're right, and then I will rest and you will wake me when it's time to get ready for tonight?"

"I will," Arthur said, taking her hand and escorting her out.

Below, in the courtyard, Maerwynn was still

looking for Gawain. She had seen the knights return and had gone out, poem in hand, to greet her returning knight. But Gawain was nowhere to be found. She saw Malagant in the distance and ran to him.

"Sir Malagant, have you seen Sir Gawain anywhere?"

"No, I haven't.

"You haven't seen him at all?"

"No. Should I have?"

"Uh, no, I guess not."

"Well, if you're looking for Gawain, I'm sure he will be at the ball tonight."

"The ball?"

"Arthur is throwing a ball tonight to celebrate the return of your sister. If you're looking for Gawain, he will probably be there."

"Actually, yes, the ball. That will be the perfect place."

"And what is that in your hand?"

"A poem."

"How lovely," the knight said and walked off.

"Yes," Maerwynn repeated. "It is lovely."

Lancelot caught up with Perceval.

"What's going on here?" Lancelot said, grabbing him by the arm.

"This whole rescue was...I don't know."

Lancelot matched Perceval's stride.

"Tell me about it."

"You know," Perceval went on, "you try to do the right thing, and then...."

"I know. I know."

"And then loyalty kicks in. I mean, loyalty to whom, to what?"

"It's a big mess. You think there's an opening...."

"And there is," Perceval said, completing the thought.

"And then you take the chance."

"And then look what happens." Perceval stopped Lancelot. "You gave me that whole talk about loyalty, and so I thought…."

"Listen, I also have my own debt to pay."

"And I have mine."

"I know. How about this? We just begin anew."

"Clear the accounts for us both," Perceval said and smiled.

"Yes."

They walked on.

"And now that we are debt free," Perceval said, "what should we do with our good names?"

"I'm already there. Tonight at the ball, I'm going to take Guinevere and I'm going to give her the greatest kiss in the history of the world."

"The greatest kiss?"

"Yes. You remember how God breathed life into Adam? I plan to challenge that, and frankly, I think that's what it will take at this point. But I have to try. And you, what will you do?"

"I will….propose marriage to Victoria."

"You think she will say yes?"

"I know she will."

They walked off, smiling.

Chapter 16

Guinevere, despite her twisting thoughts, had fallen asleep. The sun had set, and a small fire in the balcony hearth had been lit to keep the queen warm. But now it was time for the ball.

"My queen. My queen." A servant rustled her shoulder. Guin opened her eyes. "My queen. It is time to get ready."

The great hall had been prepared. The fires in the wall sconces had been shielded by yellow- and purple-colored glass so that the hall flickered in regal light. Tables with every kind of pastry and every kind of liquor had been set up to cater to the guests. The royal quartet had taken their places on the stage and began to play their melodies. And the nobility had arrived, each in their best attire to dance beneath the jewel-encrusted chandeliers. Lancelot and Perceval and the other knights stood at attention along the sidewall. Opposite them stood Victoria and Maerwynn, who was scanning the row of knights for hers. Suddenly the quartet paused and then began to play Arthur's royal theme, as the king and queen were announced.

"May I present the Royal Highnesses, King Arthur of Camelot and his beautiful Queen Guinevere."

The hall erupted in clapping and cheering. From Perceval and Lancelot came what was obligated by their duty. And from Malagant and Maerwynn distracted applause. And from Victoria the most vigorous clapping in the entire hall.

"Only the breath of God will overshadow this," Perceval whispered to Lancelot.

"If that's what it takes."

The King and Queen entered and took up their posts in a set of enormous chairs at the head of a raised table.

Conversations went around, as did small talk and murmurs, all of it combining with the music. Drinks were shared. Courtesies were exchanged, as well as investigatory looks from behind wine glasses. And then the dancing started.

The floor was cleared and lines were formed. The music then began slowly. The king and queen were paired, Perceval and Victoria, with Victoria's eyes wandering, and Lancelot with a dour maiden. Malagant and Sir Kay were mixed in, and Maerwynn was off to the side still looking for Gawain. On the surface, the lights sparkled and everyone laughed and smiled. Lancelot, as they circled, kept looking for Guinevere, trying to catch a glimpse of something, he knew not what. Partners changed. Arthur was now with Victoria. Their hands clasped, and they each put a little extra tenderness in the touch. Guinevere and Lancelot's hands were also together, but Guinevere showed not the slightest emotion.

"This afternoon, our bodies were doing what our hands are doing," he quietly said.

"For but a moment, and we were riding on a horse," she said with a straight face.

He looked away in a face of frustration. He saw Sir Kay.

"Forty-five or forty-six dragons," Sir Kay said to the pretty girl he was now with.

Lancelot and Guinevere continued to be dancing partners.

"It's called making the best of a broken world," Lancelot whispered.

"My world's not broken," she said.

Lancelot was quiet.

"Can I at least say you look beautiful this evening?" he tried.

"Isn't it your obligation to say that, your duty?" she said.

The dance continued. They moved in and then away, in and then away from each other.

"When I come in close next time, I will kiss you," Lancelot said. He was at a loss for what to say.

"You shouldn't."

When they moved in close, he blew a faint breath on her.

"Did you just breathe on me?" she said.

"Feel any emotions stirring?" he said and gave a sheepish smile.

"Not the good kind."

Partners shifted and new couples were made.

Lancelot ended up in Sir Kay's arms.

"How did this happen?" Sir Kay said.

Lancelot didn't care anymore.

"Kay, maybe you're the best I can do."

Kay grimaced. The music then concluded and the dancing stopped.

"That's it?" Kay said.

"We can still dance, if you would like?" Lancelot said, still in Kay's arms.

Kay walked off. Lancelot looked around. He saw Perceval and went over to him.

"How's the Breath of God?" Perceval asked.

Lancelot slowly shook his head.

"Where's Victoria? Did you ask her?"

"No. Not yet. Haven't had the opportunity."

They were both looking around. Lancelot saw Guinevere walking alone along the perimeter.

"You'll excuse me," Lancelot said and went after her.

He caught her in a recess and pulled her in.

"No more misdirection. Tell me," Lancelot said with a straight face.

Guinevere didn't know how to respond and stared at him with a blank face.

"Tell me," Lancelot repeated.

"Tell you what?" Guin said.

"Guinevere, tell me."

"What?"

"Just tell me."

"OK. I do have feelings for you. But I can't act on them. You wanted to know, now you know. I'm the queen."

Guinevere walked off to visit with other guests. Lancelot looked around, nodding. "At least she said what I already know," he said under his breath. Then he saw Maerwynn in the wings. Catching up to her, Lancelot took her by the arm down an adjacent corridor so no one would hear.

"What is it? Have you seen Gawain? I have this poem for him," she said.

"Yes, about Gawain."

Her eyes widened.

"Oh, is he here?"

"About Gawain." Lancelot's tone was somber. "I'm just going to come out and say it. Today, at Larimer Castle, where your sister was being held, I cut down but did not kill—I repeat, did not kill—one of the kidnappers." Maerwynn's face started to change. "And when I saw who the kidnapper was, I saw that he was Gawain."

"Not my Gawain?" She gasped.

"It looks like he was behind her kidnapping. That's why he was there, and that's why he was dressed as a member of the Wazee Tribe. I saw it with my own eyes. He was guarding her door personally."

"Not my Gawain!"

"I'm sorry."

"I sent him."

Maerwynn's knees buckled, and Lancelot caught her.

"You what?"

"I sent him myself. After the king sent you, I found

him and told him to help rescue my sister."

"He was in disguise, helping? Gawain is innocent?"

"I sent him! I sent him! To his death." Maerwynn slumped down to the ground. "I sent him to his death, and you killed him."

"He was not dead, and in fact he disappeared."

Lancelot didn't know quite what to say. Maerwynn ran off down the corridor to her room. Lancelot turned and hurried to find Perceval.

"You're in love with the king?" Perceval screamed and then muffled his voice so no one would hear. "You're in love with Arthur?" He was talking to Victoria.

"It just happened. He needed someone, and I need someone to need me," Victoria said.

"In love with Arthur?" His tone was soft and dejected.

"You don't know what he's going through. I'm sorry. I'm sorry."

"Not me?" he said quietly to himself, "Arthur?"

"I'm sorry."

Perceval walked off to the far side of the room, in a daze, his eyes glossed over. He could hardly stand. But then he grabbed Lancelot by the arm.

"Lancelot, I heard Malagant say when he was trying to pay off the Wazee that Arthur planned the whole kidnapping."

"Wait. Arthur did it? No."

"Yes, I am sure, but then we killed them all so Malagant could keep the money," Perceval said softly. He was distant.

"You sure? Gawain is innocent?"

"Gawain's name never came up?"

"Then Arthur is guilty. Perceval, you know what this means?"

"No."

"I do." And as Lancelot was about to turn away, "Perceval, go check on Maerwynn. She needs help.

She ran off to her room."

Perceval went to find Maerwynn and Lancelot scanned the crowd for Guinevere. Meanwhile, across the room:

"Victoria, tell me," Guinevere said.

"I'm sorry?"

"Tell me," Guinevere repeated.

"I don't know what you're talking about."

"Victoria, tell me."

"Your Highness, I'm sorry."

Guin looked her in the eyes.

"Tell me!"

"Fine. I'm in love with Arthur, and he had you kidnapped on purpose so that you would have an affair with Lancelot and thereby bring the downfall of Camelot."

"What?"

"What are you talking about?"

"What did you say?"

"I said…."

Guinevere turned around and charged to the middle of the room. Startled, the guests stopped talking. Where was he? Suddenly, through a gap in the crowd, she saw Lancelot. And Lancelot saw her. Both rushed.

Truly, their kiss was the shared Breath of God.

"Ah hah," Malagant called out. He swooped in from the side with Sir Kay, who grabbed Lancelot away from the queen. "Proof, witnesses, what more do we need? Take him away!"

Arthur emerged with Victoria at his side. Kay held Lancelot, and Guinevere looked around, not knowing what to do. All eyes were on her.

"Your Highness," Malagant said, "Should we also take the queen to the dungeon?"

"No," Arthur said. "I will handle her." Arthur couldn't bear the thought of Guinevere among the rats. He still had a soft spot for her. She was still his queen.

"Very well. Take him away," Malagant said.

"Is this the dance you wanted?" Kay said to Lancelot.

As Kay was about to haul Lancelot away, Perceval walked through the crowd with Maerwynn in his arms. Blood was streaming from her now-bandaged wrists. There were cries from the audience.

"She broke all the glass bottles in her room and tried to commit suicide," Perceval said and lowered her into Guinevere's arms. "But she's still breathing. I tied a cloth around her wrists," and indeed a red fabric dangled from her wounds. "She'll be fine, but she needs help."

"What caused this?" Arthur exclaimed.

"She found out the truth," Perceval said. Arthur looked at Victoria and Guinevere at Lancelot. Malagant balked. And then, with a quick glance to Lancelot before returning to address the king, Perceval drew his sword and said, "She found out it was Malagant who had kidnapped Guinevere."

This was Perceval's invention, and it was his cover.

"No!" Malagant said.

Then Perceval took his sword and slit Malagant's belt and down dropped the satchel of gold.

"Look," Perceval said. "Evidence." He picked up the satchel and took out a gold piece. "See. Evidence. And in honor of the queen and young Maerwynn, I avenge them." And Perceval drove his sword through Malagant's breastplate and into his chest, coming out clean through his back. Malagant fell over, with blood spurting out his mouth, dead. "For the honor of Camelot." Perceval then dropped his sword and knelt down on one knee. "If it needs must be, Your Highness," he said, giving himself up.

Arthur looked dumbfounded.

"If it needs must be," Lancelot echoed, still in Sir Kay's grasp.

Guinevere tended to her sister by the lamplight. Perceval's compresses had stopped the bleeding, and all that was left was to calm her nerves. Guin soaked a cloth in some cool water and laid it across Maerwynn's forehead. Her breathing was heavy but regular, and her recovery was well underway. Perceval lay on a stone slab in the courtyard, free, for no one demanded his restraint. The night was warm, and the stars were especially bright. Lancelot was in the dungeon, alone but for an old man coiled under a clump of moist hay. The condemned knight paced back and forth, kicking the hay about. Suddenly a light was lit in the hallway. Keys jangled at the outside door. And then it opened. Arthur dismissed the guard.

"Lancelot," the King said.

Lancelot appeared at the bars of his cell. The old man there with Lancelot pulled hay over himself to hide in the shadows.

"Lancelot, it appears we are really in a mess this time."

"It seems as if only I am."

"Well, the whole of the nobility watched as their queen willfully kissed a knight in front of their king. How do you think I look?"

"Like you're on the right side of these iron bars."

"Am I?"

"You can say what you like."

"Listen. Tomorrow at sunup, you will be hanged at the gallows."

Lancelot wasn't surprised.

"The people must have their justice," the knight said.

The king let out a sigh of relief.

"Then you understand. It is not I who wish you to die. It is the people who expect justice."

"Fine."

"But there is another way." The king's eyes lit up

as he said this.

"Another way? You'll forgive me if I'm not in the mood for a discussion."

"Yes. What if I left these bars open and you were to escape? We'd hunt you down, but, in the name of loyalty, I would give you a sporting chance."

"You'd let me walk out of here?"

"You were my most faithful knight, my best knight."

"Just walk out?"

"Just walk out."

Arthur took out a set of keys and unlocked Lancelot's cell.

"I will leave the outer door open, and the fields are yours."

Lancelot thought a moment. Then he reached out, grabbed the open cell door with both hands and slammed it shut.

"I will die."

"But I'm offering you freedom. Sure, we'll hunt you, but you can elude us."

"I prefer death."

"Lancelot, don't be stupid."

"No! I ran from France, and I will not run back to France. I will stay."

"I will order you to escape."

"I will defy you and stay."

"Your neck will be broken."

"Then it will be."

Arthur huffed and puffed and stormed out. Lancelot sat down. The old man threw off the hay.

"You want to die? You will not," the old man said.

"I will."

"Yes, you will, but not tomorrow."

"Old man, I have nothing and I want nothing. I might have killed my friend. I ruined Guinevere, disgraced the king, and drove Maerwynn to near suicide. What is left for me?"

"Want nothing? You want to be with Guinevere? So be with her."

"I am telling you, you will not die."

"Please. I will do as I wish."

Lancelot rolled over to try and get some sleep.

"It does not matter what you wish," the old man insisted.

"It does not matter what I wish?" Lancelot repeated under his voice. "I wish for a good breakfast, how about that?"

Lancelot covered himself in hay, and the old man stayed silent.

King Arthur made his way back down the corridors of the castle. His boots made his footsteps echo. He entered Maerwynn's room and saw the broken glass everywhere. Then he went to his room, and Guinevere was there standing over Maerwynn, who was sleeping. Perceval was off to the side, and Arthur dismissed him with a nod. Arthur and Guinevere went out onto the balcony.

"I don't have anything to say," Guinevere said and turned away.

"Why did Maerwynn do what she did?" Arthur said.

Guinevere turned to face him.

"You mean why did she try to kill herself?"

Arthur nodded.

"Because she tried to help me by sending Gawain to aid in my rescue. Perceval knows this and so does Lancelot."

"And that's it?"

"That's it? Gawain is likely dead. Lancelot thought Gawain was the kidnapper, and so he cut down his friend."

Arthur stepped back, looked away, and said under his voice, "But it was me."

Guinevere stepped toward him.

"Yes, I know. Because why? Because you wanted to

get Lancelot and I together? Why?" Arthur was quiet. "Why?" Guin repeated.

"Because I never had a chance," Arthur shouted. "I never had a chance with you. I married you knowing all this would happen." He paused. "But not Maerwynn and not Gawain. But I knew you were already lost."

"Lost?"

"To Lancelot."

"Stop. Stop. I don't want to hear it."

"It is fate."

"Just stop."

"But Guinevere...."

"If you knew this would happen and yet you did it anyway, then you are doubly responsible."

Arthur took a deep breath.

"When I married you, I did love you."

"But now your love is for Victoria?"

Arthur paused.

"You know?"

"Please stop."

"How long have you known?"

"Please stop."

Arthur was quiet. So was Guinevere.

"I can't let Lancelot out," Arthur began after a moment. "Everyone saw him kiss you."

Guinevere had her back to him and was looking out toward the darkened valley.

"And I kissed him," she said quietly.

"Listen, tomorrow, do not do anything. You do not have to."

"Stop," she said, but she had not the enthusiasm to make it sound convincing.

"Just listen. You and Lancelot will be together. I have always known it. It will happen. You do not have to do anything. He will be saved. Just wait it out."

Guin turned to face him.

"Just wait? Just wait while he is hanged? How will

it be stopped?"

"I don't know, but it will. You have nothing to worry about and neither does he. You are fated to be together, so he will be saved."

"And I just wait? No, who will save him? Who?"

"I cannot answer that."

Guinevere turned to look out over the darkened valley once more.

Day broke and the scaffolding was centered in the public square atop a raised platform. Lancelot awoke to clanging on his jail cell. It was the guard. He had brought him his breakfast. It was a large platter of eggs and potatoes and cooked vegetables and an assortment of fruits, as well as a goblet of wine. Lancelot, half disinterested, started eating. He ate the eggs and took a bite of the fruit. He rolled the potatoes around before picking one of them up in his fingers and putting it in his mouth. In doing so, his wrist shackles clanged together. He barely noticed.

"Are you ready?" the old man asked. He had been up for some time, but was still lying in the hay.

"Does it matter?" Lancelot said and went on eating.

"No, you're right. It does not matter. But may I offer you some advice?"

"If I say no, will you tell it to me anyway?" Lancelot went on eating.

"Yes. Today, do not be afraid. You have nothing to fear."

"What will happen will happen, I know."

"There is no death for you this morning."

"Please, old man. Look at me. Don't tell me I will not die."

Lancelot held up his wrist irons.

"Oh, you will die, but not today. You heard that."

The two prisoners heard keys jangling at the outside door. Then the old man quickly threw off his hay and emerged out of the darkness. Lancelot's eyes widened.

"Merlin! You've been in here? What for?"

"Just listen. The guard is coming. You will be with Guinevere. You cannot die today."

"I cannot?"

"Fate has spoken. You cannot die today."

The guard came in and started to unlock Lancelot's cell. Lancelot looked at the Merlin, who was now in the shadows. The guard swung Lancelot's door open and reached for the knight. Lancelot stepped forward before looking at Merlin once more. He paused. "One moment," he said to the guard. Then Lancelot slowly knelt down to his tray and picked up his wine goblet. He looked into the red wine, and then he quickly tilted the goblet up to his chest and pressed it flush against his clothing. The red wine at first stayed in the cup, as it was sealed, trapped against the fabric, before leaking out. Lancelot then tilted the cup back and threw it into the corner. A circular red stain was imprinted over his heart. It was a large solitary red dot. Then he went out with the guard. But before leaving the jail, he looked back to Merlin, who once again said, "There's no need."

"But why are you here?" Lancelot called out.

"I have been waiting for you," came Merlin's voice from out of sight.

Lancelot was led out of the jail and marched through a crowd that had gathered by the doorway. The crowd was silent. They couldn't believe what they were seeing. Even more people had encircled the scaffolding. A masked executioner was standing alone atop the woodwork, making sure the noose was tight and checking the sturdiness of the apparatus. Guinevere, wearing a dark cloak, was walking out of a side passageway, but instead of turning towards the crowd, she ducked down a small alleyway. A coach was there waiting. Perceval came from around front.

"The horses are tied in, and Maerwynn's inside."

Guin looked in the cabin, and her sister was there wrapped in a blanket, sleeping, as she was still recovering. Sitting next to her was a man, hunched over, and in the partial light she could see it was Gawain. Still in pain from the leg wound, he was nevertheless alive.

"There are no dragons," Gawain said.

Guin nodded and then turned to Perceval.

"Good, now come on."

They walked toward the crowd.

Lancelot was led up to the scaffolding. All was silent. The executioner read a formal declaration. There were some muffled noises from the crowd. But all was still, motionless.

Arthur looked on from a nearby balcony. Victoria was at his side.

Guinevere and Perceval hid behind a pillar. The crowd had been packed in tight, so they couldn't get any closer without risking being seen. Guinevere stood with her back to the pillar. Perceval peeked out.

"What can you see?" Guinevere said.

"Not much. There're two figures up there. One appears to be Lancelot."

"Appears?" Guin said. "Maybe it's a double."

Perceval looked closer.

"No. It's him."

"I was told he would be saved. I was told it was fate."

"Well, nothing's happening."

"I was told it would be stopped."

"No one is doing anything to stop it."

Guinevere took a deep breath. She couldn't watch. Arthur, from his balcony, looked on. He watched the perimeter of the crowd.

"Where will our kingdom be? Where will our castle be?" Victoria asked.

Arthur wasn't paying attention. He was looking for

the hand of fate.

"Arthur," Victoria repeated. "Our castle, if not here, where will it be?"

Arthur, without taking his eyes away, said "Larimer Castle."

"What?"

"Larimer Castle. I will govern the Wazee Tribe. It has been worked out. They are waiting for me."

Victoria sighed and Arthur went back to concentrating on the crowd.

"Still nothing," Perceval said.

Guinevere couldn't watch. She looked around the perimeter.

"What did you say last night?" she said, thinking back.

"When?"

"When you killed Malagant."

"Oh. If it needs must be."

"If it needs must be," she said to herself.

She started to nod.

"Is there anything more obvious than fate?" she said.

"What?" Perceval said, still looking at the scaffolding. "Why hasn't anything happened?"

"Because I haven't done it yet," she said.

Guinevere stood up straight, took a deep breath, and started walking toward the scaffolding, making her way through the people. As she got closer, that's when she saw it, the large red mark on Lancelot's chest. And a moment later, their eyes met.

ABOUT THE AUTHOR

Zelko Smith is the writing team of Peter and Aaron Gabbani, with Zelko being their middle name. Between them, they have a J.D. and two masters degrees. They write in the middle of the night.

atriscopress@gmail.com.

Printed in Great Britain
by Amazon